SUGAR PETITE

by
MILDRED L. McVEA

Photographs from family album
Other illustrations by the author

Copyright
MILDRED L. MCVEA
1959 and 1989

To
PEARL LOBDELL McVEA,
the original "Sugar Petite,"
whose memories live on
in these pages

For Susanna

From Dae With love

Christmas 1990

Contents

Foreword		vii
1.	Petite and Julia	1
2.	The Family	10
3.	Eva	16
4.	Old Friends in the House	23
5.	Papa	36
6.	In the Tree House	41
7.	Pinkie	49
8.	The Sugar Bowl Game	59
9.	On the Levee	70
10.	Christmas Day	80
11.	"Dolly Madison's" Funeral	91
12.	A Prayer for Pinkie	100
13.	The Hurricane	114
14.	The Gypsies	126
15.	New Happiness in the Big House	141
16.	Petite Meets Charlie	149
17.	The Fruit Peddler	158
18.	Petite Makes a Decision	163
Epilogue		169
Songs and Games from Belle Vale		170
Belle Vale Family Records		181

Foreword

Across the Mississippi river from Louisiana's capital city of Baton Rouge the fertile delta still stretches in mile after mile of green sugar cane. Many plantations remain of those first established more than a century and a half ago; but many, too, are gone, their land eaten away by the changing banks of the river that once gave them life, the descendents of their owners scattered to different parts of the country.

Such is the case with the plantation described in this book. Belle Vale once existed just as it is described in the story you are about to read, although today a careful search is required to find its location. Its home site and much of its land have been swallowed by the river, but the site can be reached by traveling from Baton Rouge across the Mississippi river to Port Allen on Interstate 10, exiting onto Highway 415 at Exit 151. Continue north on 415 through Lobdell and follow 415 as it winds under Highway 190 and to the river. Near the river Highway 415 is also named Plantation Avenue. When you reach the levee turn right and you will be on old Belle Vale property.

In the original 1959 edition of *Sugar Petite*, only first names were given. At the end of this edition several pages of Belle Vale family records have been added. For further information about the Lobdells and the McVeas (Charlie's family), it is suggested that the reader consult the excellent regional history, *The Plains and The People*, by Virginia Lobdell Jennings.

The servants in the story are all taken from real life, as are the games and songs enjoyed by the children and the

Foreword

background against which the characters move, and all were drawn from accounts given by those who could still remember in vivid detail. To be sure, some of the events related have been fabricated and others simply embroidered to weave an interesting pattern around the solid foundation of fact. For example, Julia was "willed" to the white family for the reason given, but her Indian descent is an added touch. The old albino, Pinkie, did give to Petite the nickname she loved, but the trip to the cabin is an imaginary one. The gypsies did come, and the hurricane did strike although probably not in the spring. A few liberties have been taken with the ages of the children, to enhance the story as originally planned and to confine it to one year (1886) in the life of a young girl growing up on a sugar plantation.

Petite first met her Charlie when she was about this age. Throughout a long lifetime she kept alive her memories of Belle Vale and it was from the stories of her childhood, as told to six adoring grandchildren, that this book came into being. The wonderful way of life here presented has become little more than a memory. Customs and attitudes have changed as they ever must, but the picture of a growing family holds features that are the same in any age. It is hoped that this story will find a place in the hearts, not only of other *petites* (French word for "little girls") who may see their own feelings reflected in its pages, but of all who find enrichment of the present in an occasional retreat into the past.

MILDRED L. MCVEA

Baton Rouge, Louisiana
Summer, 1989

Sugar Petite

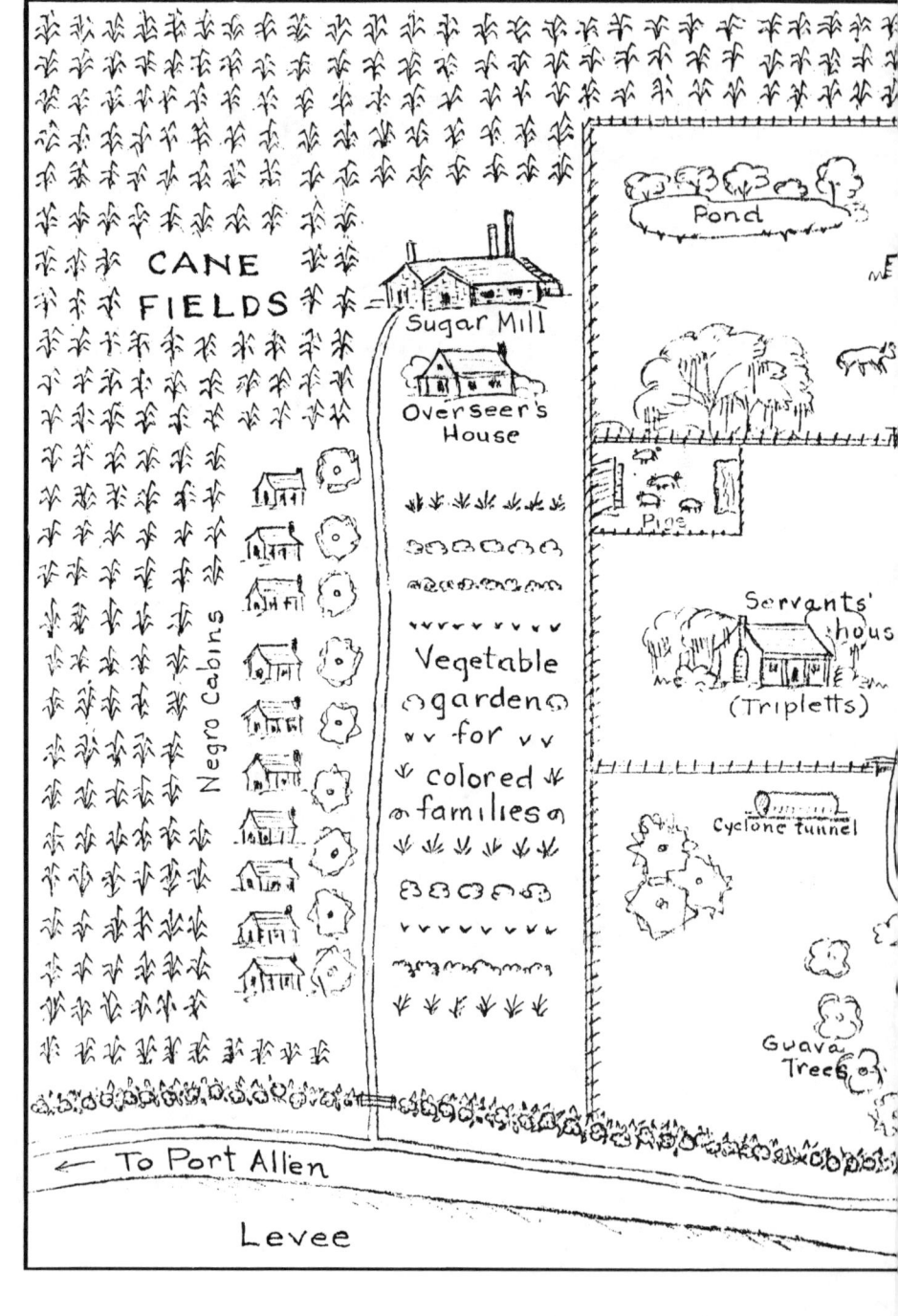

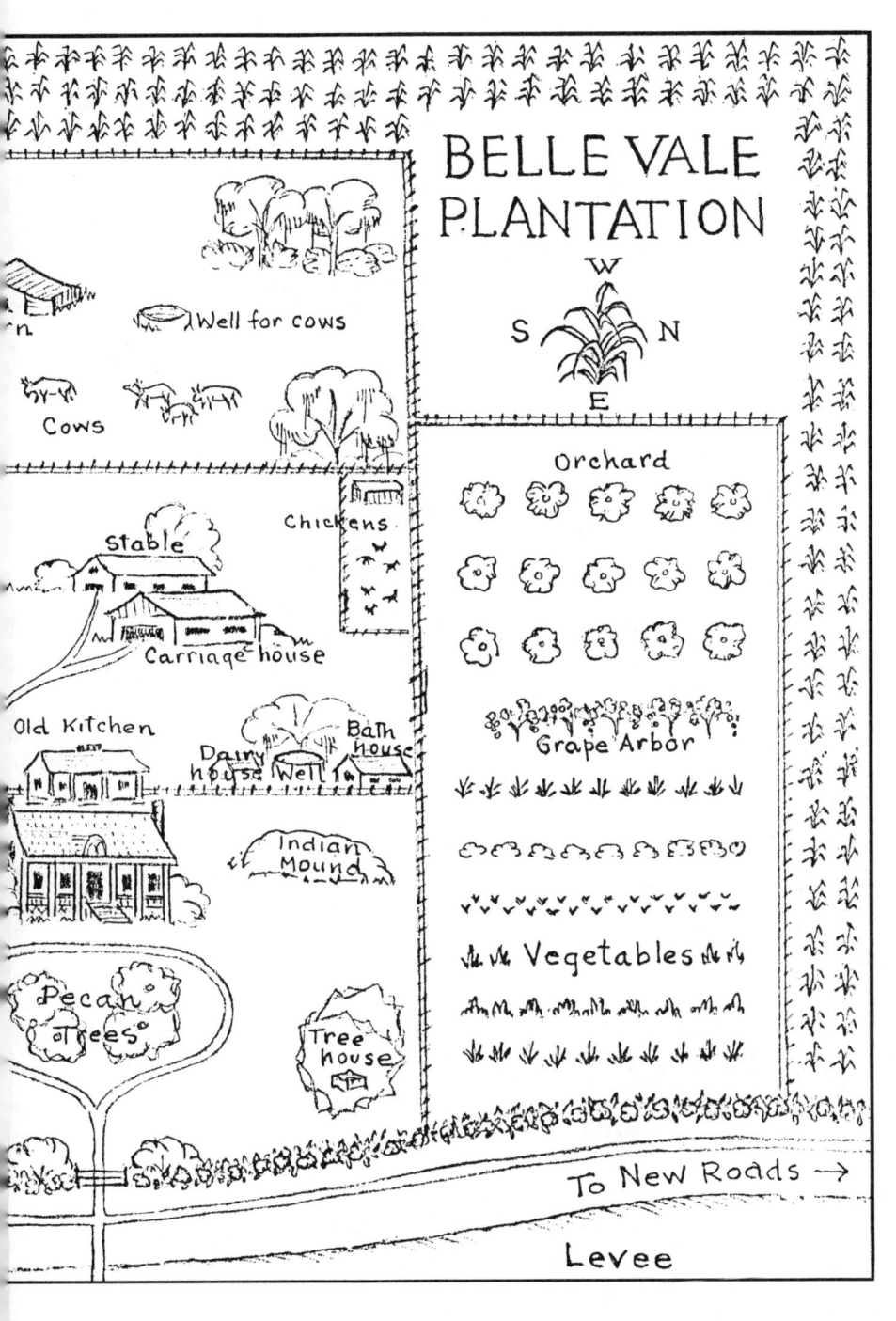

1. Petite and Julia

The bedroom in the large old house was warm and comfortable, and quiet except for the gay crackling sound of the fire in the hearth and the soft voice of the dusky young figure kneeling beside it:

> "*She grind de meal,*
> *She gimme de husk,*
> *She bake de bread,*
> *She gimme de crust.*
> *Juba, Juba,*
> *Juba dis an' Juba dat,*
> *Juba killed de yaller cat.*
> *Ole Aunt Kate!*"

It was a strange little song—recited rather than really sung—a measured, monotonous chant with the voice raised about two notes at the end of the last word. To anyone else it might have sounded weird and completely lacking in meaning, but to the little girl lying on the

Sugar Petite

day bed it was the most beautiful and welcome sound she had heard in months.

"*If I lie very still,*" she thought, "*and keep my eyes shut tight, maybe she won't go away, even if she is just a dream. It's Julia and she's singing our own special song—the one we always sing when we want something.*"

She smiled to herself, letting her mind wander back to a time, not so very many years before, soon after the colored child had come to live with the family in the big white house. The tiny Julia had brought the song with her to the delight of the white children, who decided at once that it had something to do with "voodoo" and held a magic power all its own, known only to those versed in the ways of Black Magic. "Juba dis an' Juba dat." Why had Juba killed "de yaller cat"? And who was "ole Aunt Kate"? No one could explain the mystery of the fascinating words.

Petite and Julia had discovered almost immediately that they were "twins," sharing the same birthday as well as the same number of years, and the feeling of closeness that resulted was marred only by the difference in their color and the knowledge that they could never love each other as equals. It was here that the song "Juba" had played its comical and, at the same time, pathetic little part. If it really could work Black Magic, the two children had decided, and if they tried very hard and were solemn about it, maybe they could change the color of Julia's skin to a beautiful white. Then they could be twins, really for true.

Petite had fought down a feeble twinge of conscience which told her that Papa would not approve of her playing with Black Magic. Then, with curly brown head

Petite and Julia

and inky black one close together, they had plotted their experiment. The plan finally decided upon was this: they would hold hands and, keeping their eyes tightly closed, would recite the verse three times while slowly turning in a circle—first to the right, then to the left, and finally to the right again. This, Julia had said, would make the "voodoos" take notice and, at the same time, would keep them from getting dizzy. At the end of the third verse, they would get on their knees and raise their arms above their heads, waving their hands while singing the last words, "Ole Aunt Kate," just to please that mysterious lady, whoever she might be. After that they would open their eyes and see what had happened.

Of course they had emerged from the experience two sadder and wiser little girls, though perhaps a bit relieved over not having to make disturbing explanations to the rest of the family. At any rate, the little song had taken on a special meaning for them. From that day on, it had been a kind of secret signal to each other in time of stress or longing, even now that they were big girls, thirteen years old, and were no longer allowed the closer companionship of their younger years.

"*It's not a dream,*" thought Petite, "*and I know what she wants. She's waiting for me to wake up.*" Reality was beginning to take form again, and the picture of the past few days was fitting itself together in neat little pieces like a simple jigsaw puzzle. She needn't worry about waking up and finding herself miles away from her beloved Belle Vale. This time she was sure that it wasn't a dream.

She knew that she was on the day bed in Mamma and Papa's room where she had been undressed and ten-

Sugar Petite

derly "tucked in" the night before, after the long trip up from New Orleans. Somehow she couldn't remember much about the trip itself. She had still been feeling ill and weak, and it all seemed just a confused, blurry memory—the luxurious and brightly lighted steamboat, the churning vibration of the great wheels as they plowed their way up the Mississippi, the comfort of the clean cabin bunk and, above all, the glorious feeling of contentment every time she looked at Papa and knew that he was taking her home.

How could she *ever* have thought that she wanted to go away to school? Sister Lena, only two years older than she, had liked it from the first day. Everyone knew that Valence Institute was a wonderful school; and Aunt Lou and Aunt Lydia, in whose home they stayed, had been as kind and sweet as could be. It was just that it was all so far away and so terribly different from the happy plantation life she had always known. She had tried hard to be brave. Maybe she would have won the battle within herself if it hadn't been for the lingering sick spell that had finally brought an anxious Papa to her rescue.

Two months that had seemed like years! But now it was all over. For the time being, at least, she was safe at home. Suddenly she was surprised to find that she no longer felt miserable and ill, but rather warm and cozy and very happy inside. At the same time, she noticed that Julia had stopped her singing.

Petite opened her eyes and looked across the room. Julia was sitting back on her heels, no longer paying any attention to the fire she had been sent in to tend. Her face was turned with a very worried expression toward the bed on which her little mistress lay. She was

Petite and Julia

a pleasant looking young girl, small for her age and of delicate build. Her skin was a soft, light brown. Her nose was straight and well shaped beneath a pair of expressive, dark eyes. She wore her jet-black hair caught to the back of her head in a tight little knot.

There was no doubt that Julia was different from the rest of the colored folk. Petite knew that this was because her father's mother had been a full-blooded Houma Indian. To the girl this strain of different blood had brought only a certain air of withdrawal, of gentle and solemn acceptance of whatever came her way. It was in her father and his two huge sons that the savage broke loose from time to time. Old Gus was one of Papa's best field hands during the week, when he left whiskey alone. But every Saturday night, when pay day had put the necessary money in his pockets, he came home to his cabin loud and rough and sometimes even wild. It was whispered among the children that he had beaten Julia's gentle mother and had been cruel to her even when she was ill. That was why, when she knew she was going to die, she had sent her little daughter to Mamma with the message that she was "willing" her to the family and begging them to take care of her and keep her from harm.

Of course, no one dared ask questions about all this. Children were not supposed to know such things. At any rate, Mamma had shown no hesitation when the small stranger arrived at the back door, her few poor belongings tied tightly in an old quilt. She had ordered a cot set up for her in the children's room; and there she had remained, a playmate at first and, for the past few years, a valuable little maid.

Sugar Petite

"Mornin', Julia." Petite's voice sounded queer and weak; and when she tried to lift her head, she found with dismay that it felt much better back on the soft pillow where it had been the moment before. The little colored girl was beside her in a flash, her face flooded with a sunny smile.

"Lawd, Miss Pearl," she said, "Ah thought you was never gonna wake up! Yo' mamma say to let you sleep all mornin' if you wants to—but you look so pale and you sleep so long—" She lowered her eyes in a gesture of shame. "Ah reckon Ah shouldn't a sung so loud."

"I'm glad you did," said Petite. "I didn't want to sleep all day and, anyway, I'm all right now, truly I am—just a little tired, I guess, from the long trip home."

She sat up in bed and hugged her knees as she looked very seriously at her companion. "Julia, why did you call me *Miss Pearl* just now? I don't look that much older, do I?"

Julia shook her head. "No'm," she answered softly, "you don't look no older at all. It's jes' dat sence you's growed up an' been away to school—well, 'Aunt Harriet' say . . ."

"Oh, bother 'Aunt Harriet'!" interrupted Petite, knowing how the old colored woman liked to boss the others. "I'm not grown up at all. And really, Julia," she lowered her voice almost to a whisper, "I'm not sure that I want to be, ever. It was so *awful* being away from home. Everyone was good to me, but I was so lonesome I just couldn't stand it. And after I got sick . . ."

She began to cough, and lay back on her pillow with her eyes closed. Julia wasn't sure whether it was from weakness or to hide the tears she had seen shining there.

Petite and Julia

"Now, you see," said Julia solemnly, "we's gone an' done it! Yo' mamma say you shouldn't talk too much— an' she make me promise to come tell her de minute you wake up. Her an' Miss Carrie both busy fixin' fo' Thankgivin' tomorrow." She started for the door but turned with a grin. "One thing Ah reckon Ah better tell you befo' Ah go. When you see Eva, don' let on you notice 'bout her face lookin' bad."

"Her face?" repeated Petite, sitting up again at the mention of her little sister. "Whatever happened to her face?"

"Well, it was sho'ly a turrible thing." Julia came back to stand beside the bed. "You see, de young folks all had dere pecan money. De trees was jes' loaded dis year, an' dey all had mo' dimes en you could count . . ."

"And I wasn't here!" exclaimed Petite. Each fall Papa let the children have as their own all the pecans they could gather under Belle Vale's many trees, and these they were allowed to sell to the colored hands on pay day for ten cents a hundred.

"Ev'ybody was waitin' fo' de next fruit peddler to come to de house," Julia went on, "an' by-'n-by one come —but you know what? It warn't dat nice Mr. Ragusa dat ginerly come up from New Orleans. Dis man say Mr. Ragusa, he's sick; an' dat him's his cousin come in his place. Ah knowed de minute Ah seed him dat he warn't up to no good." She paused and looked around uneasily, as if speaking of an evil spirit who might be listening.

"Go on," urged Petite. "What happened?"

"Well, dis man have some fancy lookin' jahs in his basket dat he say is a fine kind of cream fo' ladies' faces. He say it's sure to make de skin purty an' white; take

Sugar Petite

off all de freckles an' spots an' ev'ything. Miss Carrie say, 'No, thank you, don' none of us care fo' none,' but you know what dat Eva do?"

"She didn't buy some?" gasped Petite.

Julia nodded her head. "Dat's jes' ezzacly what she do. Whilse de chillun was buyin' dere fruit an' 'Johnny Crook' an' 'Stage Plank,' she slip him all de money she have an' take a jah of dat stuff whilse nobody wasn't lookin'."

"And then?" Petite was wide-eyed with interest.

"Well, den she hide it in her room an' dat night she rub it all over her face to make her beautiful whilse she's sleep." Julia grinned. "It take off all de freckles, all right, but it mos' take off all de skin, too. Aftah ev'ybody was in bed, it staht in to burn. An' dere she was, a-jumpin' aroun' an' a-yellin' fo' somebody to 'Git it off! Git it off!' You shoulda seed yo' pa! He's madder'n Ah ever seed him befo'. Directly he give her sumpin' to make it quit hurtin', an' it's better now . . . but she still look like sumpin' boiled."

"Poor little Eva," said Petite. "What a dreadful way to be punished! She just wants so much to be grown up!"

"Ah'll say she do." Julia shook her head in disapproval. "An' her jes' nine year old! You know what she say to me de other day? 'Julia', she say, 'Ah's nine year old now, an' Ah think it 'bout time fo' you to staht callin' me *Miss*.'"

Petite laughed. "What did you tell her?"

"Ah tell her Ah'll call her *Miss* when her mamma say to. An' she stick out her tongue at me, an' flounce outa de room jes' as sassy as you please! She's sho' diffunt from you, all right."

Petite and Julia

"Well, anyway," Petite assured her, "don't let me hear any more *Miss Pearl* 'til I tell you myself. I may not be so *little* anymore, but my name is still *Petite*, do you hear? That's what I've been called ever since I can remember, and that's the way I want it. Now you run find my Mamma."

2. The Family

After Julia left to look for Mamma, Petite settled back on the pillow and let her eyes wander slowly over the familiar old room. Directly opposite her was her parents' huge double bed, now neatly made for the day with its faded but still handsome patchwork quilt and white ruffled pillow-shams hiding the two large feather pillows. Close beside it was the small four-poster baby bed in which nine babies had each had a turn. It now belonged to little Willie, the two year old darling of the household, who had somehow earned for himself the rather startling nickname of "Nootsie." That he was a spoiled little darling was not surprising, since he was only the third son in the large family and had put in his appearance after a straight run of five little girls. Petite wondered where he was now. Somewhere in the house, she supposed, being played with by five year old Bena, who still regarded him as a delightful new toy produced solely for her amusement.

She glanced to the other side of the room where sunlight was filtering in through the white curtained windows, in spite of the fact that their shutters had been closed to lend as much darkness as was possible on such a beautiful day. Between the windows was the fireplace, and on the mantel a large gold clock pointed its hands to the amazing hour of ten. What a dreadful lazy bones she had been! No wonder Julia had begun to wonder if she would ever open her eyes.

Petite loved Mamma and Papa's room, with its well-

The Family

worn carpeted floor and practical furniture, the tremendous armoire in which they kept their clothes, and the old rocking chair in which so many babies had been sung to sleep. But most of all she loved the day bed on which she was lying. She knew that her being there now was a very special sign of her parents' love; that they had wanted her close to them during her first night at home, where they could watch her every move and be sure that she was all right, just as they had always done when one of the children was not feeling well. She wondered how many times they had listened through the night for the whimper of a sick child lying on this bed, and how many little aches and pains had been eased because of the knowledge that Mamma and Papa were close at hand. Even now, just being there seemed, as if by magic, to chase away every unhappy feeling she had ever known. She smiled and snuggled deeper in bed with a long, contented sigh.

The old day bed, she thought, was important for another reason. In a way it was the most important piece of furniture in the whole house, for on it had been born all of Mamma's babies—all, that is, except Brother Jimmie, who had completely upset family tradition by arriving in a cabin back in the canebrakes where Mamma had fled in fear of shells from Yankee gunboats during the War. Petite knew that Jimmie had never forgiven the Union Army for causing him to be the only one of the children to be born away from Belle Vale. Oh well, they should all remember that, on the whole, their family and the plantation, too, had been lucky to escape any real harm at the hands of the Yankees. She supposed things were somewhat harder now than before the War.

Sugar Petite

She knew that there were fewer servants than during slavery times and more worries for Papa in the management of his business. But they were all well and happy, and she wouldn't exchange one minute of life as she knew it for all the glories of the past.

The sound of footsteps coming down the hall interrupted her trend of thought. The next instant Mamma and Sister Carrie hurried into the room. Carrie was holding little Nootsie in her arms, and Bena was following close at her heels. Mamma folded Petite for a moment in her soft arms, while Carrie leaned down to give her a kiss. Petite had forgotten how beautiful they were. She noticed for the first time how much alike they looked, with their fine, white skin in such startling contrast to their black hair and dark brown eyes. But Mamma's hair was beginning to show streaks of gray, and there were tiny lines in her once smooth face. After all, she was already a grandmother, while Carrie was only twenty-two and still radiantly untouched by the hand of time. Nootsie was kicking and wiggling in Carrie's arms, letting forth a series of gleeful little squeals, while Bena promptly climbed up on the bed to snuggle close beside her on the pillow. What a wonderful welcome home!

"Now, let me have a good look at you," Mamma was saying. "You were so sleepy and worn out last night, we just bundled you into bed without even turning up the lamp. Jimmie says he never did figure out whether you were awake or asleep during the drive back to the house from the landing."

She took her little daughter's face in her hands and studied it closely for a minute. "A little pale and thin,"

The Family

she announced, "but 'Aunt Rachel's' good cooking will have you fat and rosy again in no time."

"An' I saved you a piece of my 'Stage Plank'," murmured Bena, burying her tiny nose against her sister's shoulder.

Petite gave her a hard squeeze. She knew that this was a real love offering, for the hard, sweet gingercake was a rare and special treat to the children, not to be parted with lightly. "Thank you, precious," she said, "I know that's exactly what I need."

"Now," said Mamma, "tell me all about everything in New Orleans. How is Lena getting along at school?"

"Oh, she's just wonderful, Mamma! She loves the school, and she's so popular with all the girls. Aunt Lou and Aunt Lydia say she's a real young lady already. She's wearing her hair put-up now, and she's so pretty . . ." Her face clouded. She was going to miss her vivacious sister if Papa decided to let her stay at home.

Mamma sensed the change in her mood and hurried on to another subject. "Your father and Jimmie are out in the fields, but they'll be in to see you just as soon as they come back to the house. The cane crop was fine this year, and they're trying to get it all cut and hauled to the sugar mill before the winter rains begin. Jimmie is such a help to your father," she added proudly. Petite smiled proudly, too. After several years at Louisiana State University, across the river in Baton Rouge, Jimmie was now at home to stay, sharing in the management of the plantation. Papa had even been able to let the overseer go, now that he had his own son to work with him. It was hard to think of her teasing, good looking brother as a real business man; but, like it or not, they

Sugar Petite

were all growing up—at least, the older ones were. Brother Johnny and sister Belle were both married now and had left Belle Vale to start families of their own. How funny that Nootsie was uncle to a baby girl exactly his own age!

Suddenly Petite missed her other little sister. "Where's Eva?" she asked, looking all around the room as if expecting to find her hiding behind a piece of furniture.

Mamma frowned and it was Carrie who answered. "Eva is . . . er . . . being sort of difficult just now. She had a little accident about a week ago and . . ."

"I know," said Petite, "Julia told me all about it." And then the pitiful truth became clear. "She doesn't want me to see her face! Oh, poor little Eva!"

But Mamma was not so sympathetic. "She's being very stubborn and foolish about the whole thing," she said. "Her face is much better now, but she still hides when anyone comes to the house, and cries if she thinks anyone is looking at her too hard."

"Well, you can't much blame her," interceded Petite. "She's feeling hurt and ashamed all at the same time. But I don't want her to be afraid of me, and I do want to see her. Please don't tell her I know about her face," she begged. "Just tell her I want awfully much to see her and . . . and that I've brought her something pretty from New Orleans. Tell her it will hurt my feelings if she doesn't come."

"Very well, I'll try again," sighed Mamma, making it quite clear that Eva had already refused once to come in to bid her welcome. "I'll send Indie with the children to look for her. I think she's playing alone somewhere outside, maybe in the tree house. But now . . ." her

The Family

worried look changed back to a happy one, "how would you like to have Julia help you bathe and move into your own room? I think you'd be more comfortable back in your own big bed."

"But I'd rather get up and dress," Petite objected.

"Not until tomorrow," said Mamma firmly. "Tomorrow is Thanksgiving and will be a full day. Johnny and Belle are coming with their families to spend the day with us, and we don't want them to find you looking like a ghost. You stay in bed for the rest of today, and I believe that by tomorrow you'll be feeling quite like yourself again."

"All right, Mamma, if you say so," Petite replied obediently, and Mamma leaned over to kiss her again. "That's our Sugar Petite," she said.

3. Eva

When Julia returned to the room, she was carrying a tray holding a large cup of *café au lait,* a plate of tiny biscuits and a pitcher of syrup.

" 'Aunt Rachel' say it's too late fo' breakfast an' too early fo' dinnah," she announced, "so jes' you eat dis to hold you whilse you's waitin'. An' from de smell of de gumbo she's makin', it's gonna be a dinnah wuth waitin' fo'." She sniffed the air in appreciation. "Shrimp an' okra, an' it's got de whole house smellin' good!" She waited for Petite to prop herself up in bed, then set the tray across her knees.

Petite took a long, deep breath. The food smelled and looked delicious. No one could drip coffee as strong and black as "Aunt Rachel's," or bake biscuits as light. And, of course, nowhere in the whole world was the cane syrup as good as that from Belle Vale's own sugar mill. She took a sip of the coffee and ran an approving tongue around her lips. M-m-m, it was good! People could talk all they wanted to about the fine cooking in New Orleans, but it never tasted like this.

Julia was now bustling about in the next room. The Girls' Bedroom opened off Mamma and Papa's room and also had a door that led to a small porch with steps going down to the back yard. Through this entrance the servants brought water to the bedrooms for bathing during the winter months when the bath house, close to the well in the back yard, was too cold for use. A bowl and pitcher on the washstand in each bedroom was used for the simpler daily bathing, but for a real "all over bath" a large tub was brought in and placed before the fireplace.

Petite heard Julia come and go several times and could imagine her getting everything ready—the buckets of hot water carried from the kitchen, the soap and large soft towel laid out beside the tub. She could hear her humming to herself as she worked. Dear, patient, little Julia—she was happy to have her to wait on again.

But just then another thought crowded everything else from her mind. She had sent word to Eva that she had brought her something pretty from New Orleans. What was it going to be? She had gone shopping several times with Aunt Lou and Aunt Lydia and had stopped to admire all the pretty things in the shop windows, especially those on Royal Street with their fascinating displays of jewelry and old silver, but not one thing had she bought. She had been saving all of her spending money to buy Christmas presents for the family when the time drew nearer. Oh, why had she sent that sudden and foolish message to tempt her stubborn little sister? She just *had* to think of something!

All at once she knew what it must be. She stretched out her hand and looked hard at the small mosaic ring encircling one of her fingers. Aunt Lydia had given it to her when she was sick. Her heart skipped a beat as a momentary wave of regret swept over her. It was a pretty little ring, although Aunt Lydia had said that it really wasn't worth very much—just something she had found packed among the things saved from the time when she, too, was young. Petite knew she would never forget how much it had meant to her when she was sick and

Sugar Petite

lonely to know that her aunt loved her enough to give it to her, but she didn't really need it now. She was well and happy again, and it was Eva who was miserable and hurt and feeling apart from everyone. She would give the ring to her. She felt sure that Aunt Lydia would understand.

A short time later she was lying, clean and refreshed, in one of the two big double beds in the Girls' Room. It was a large, cheery room with three windows. Its furniture was similar to that in the other bedroom— the heavy armoire which served as a closet, a dresser between two of the windows, and a marble-topped washstand on which was placed a handsome, handpainted set of bowl and pitcher. Over the fireplace hung a portrait of Grandmother. The mantel shelf held an assorted array of feminine bric-a-brac, some of them useful and some of purely sentimental value.

A few years ago, the room had been shared by the four older sisters (the younger children occupied a room of their own opening off the other end of their parents' room) but now that Belle was married and Lena away at school, Petite and Carrie would have it all to themselves. It seemed quiet and lonely now. It was going to be very different from the years when there were two girls in each bed, with all the fun and laughter and secrets whispered in the dark.

Julia had finished tidying up and had just left to report to her mistress when there was a loud burst of commotion outside the door. A moment later, the missing Eva was all but shoved into the room by a triumphant and grinning Indie.

Indie (a shortened form of her real name which was

Eva

Indiana Territory Billings) was the little children's nurse, and a more startling looking companion it would be hard to imagine. She was tall and very black, with huge hands and feet and a most amazing pair of eyes which she rolled about to add emphasis to the apparently endless supply of songs, stories and games stored up in her queer looking head. But if her eyes were amazing, even more so was her mouth, for she possessed a set of large, white and very protruding buckteeth which looked as if they were ready to fly from her face to take a bite out of any unsuspecting bystander.

On only one occasion, however, were they ever known to have been as dangerous as they looked, and that was many years ago. One hapless day, during a wild game of chase which they were all playing on the big gallery in front of the house, Lena had suddenly reversed her direction and had run headlong into Indie, whose two front teeth had sunk deep into her forehead. Petite could still remember every detail—the children all screaming at the sight of the blood, and poor Indie wringing her huge hands as she cried over and over, "Oh, Lawdy, Lawdy, Ah done bit Lena!" Papa had stopped the bleeding with a handful of cobwebs gathered from the gallery ceiling, and fortunately the wound had healed without delay. But from that day on, Indie's teeth had been regarded by all the children with a great deal of cautious respect.

All of this crossed Petite's mind now, as she looked from jubilant black Indie to red-faced little Eva, standing with lowered eyes in front of her bed.

"Good mawnin', Petite," Indie was saying loudly. "We's sure glad to have you home. An' here's Eva Ah

Sugar Petite

done foun'. She was hidin' under de ole kitchen buildin', but Ah done fetched her out."

"I was *not* hiding," insisted Eva. "I was fixing the doll houses. And I was coming to see you anyway, Petite." She raised her eyes to look at her sister, who sent her a warm smile and was rewarded with a feeble little grin.

"I'm sure you were," said Petite, "and I've been waiting for you . . . Now, you run along, Indie, and play with the little children. I'm glad to see you, too, but Eva and I have things to talk about."

Indie backed out of the door, bowing as she went, and Petite and Eva were left alone.

"*I just have to say something about her face,*" thought Petite. "*It's even redder and worse looking than I imagined. She's sure to think it's funny if I don't notice it at all . . .*" The next moment she heard herself asking: "How'd you ever get yourself so sunburned, Eva? Did you go to sleep in the sun?"

A sudden look of relief passed over the crimson little face. "I sure did," she answered quickly, "and it blistered something awful. But . . . but Papa gave me some salve to put on it, and it's lots better now." She ran her fingers cautiously over the tender looking young skin. "I think it'll be all right again soon."

"Of course it will," Petite assured her. "Now come here to the side of the bed. I have something for you. Did anyone tell you?" Then, as Eva nodded and came to stand close beside her, "Here, hold out your hand."

She drew the ring off her own finger and slipped it onto the little girl's. Their hands, she noticed, were nearly the same size. Eva *was* growing up, in spite of them all.

"It's a real lady's ring," Petite said importantly. "It was Aunt Lydia's when she was a young lady, and she gave it to me when I was sick . . . but now I've decided I want you to have it."

"Oh, it's *beautiful!*" Eva pronounced the words softly, turning her hand to admire the delicately patterned colors of the ring. Then, suddenly, she looked straight at Petite. "Why are you giving it to me?" she asked. "Why don't you want to keep it for yourself?"

This was such an unexpected reaction that for a minute Petite didn't know what to say. She couldn't tell her it was a bribe to get her to come to her, and she didn't want her to know that she felt sorry for her because of her face.

"Why, I just wanted you to have it," she said slowly, feeling for words as she went. "I . . . I missed you and wanted to bring you something from New Orleans . . . and I didn't have a chance to buy you anything. I'd just rather give it to you than keep it myself, that's all."

Eva kept looking at the ring. It would be quite the most beautiful, as well as the most grownup, thing she had ever owned. But should she keep it? Would her sister be sorry later that she had given it to her? The colors glowed and seemed to beckon to her. Petite had said that she wanted her to have it more than she wanted it herself . . .

Finally she looked up and met her sister's eyes. She reached out her hand, wearing the new ring, and touched Petite's bare one. "Thank you, Petite," she said seriously.

Sugar Petite

"You're a good sister, and I'm very glad that you're home."

Then she turned and walked slowly from the room.

4. Old Friends in the House

Thanksgiving dawned a perfect day. At first Petite wasn't sure just what had awakened her, and then she was conscious of Nootsie's chirping in the next room. The family often laughingly said that he was just like a little bird, with his own special morning song to start each new day. He was singing it now, lying in his bed and making cheerful little sounds to himself while waiting for someone to take him up. Mamma must still be asleep, thought Petite, for if she left without him, the happy sounds always quickly changed into an angry roar. What a funny little bird, to be able to roar as well as to sing!

Carrie was awake, too. Already dressed, she was standing in front of the mirror over the washstand, combing and arranging her long dark hair. Petite watched her a few minutes, wondering how it must feel to be a grown young lady, so sure of oneself in all the ways of the grownup world. Her sister's slender fingers moved swiftly and surely to roll the long strands of hair into a smooth coil at the back of her head. Petite's own fingers were awkward and fumbling with hairpins, and she was always quite out of patience by the time she finished trying to arrange her hair with them. And then it seldom stayed in place for any length of time. That was why she still liked to wear it in a braid or caught with a ribbon at the back of her neck. Long hair was a terrible bother, no matter how hard you tried to learn to fix it.

Carrie turned and saw that she was being watched.

Sugar Petite

"You awake, too?" she asked softly. "It's still early to get up, you know. I thought I'd get started before Mamma this morning, since I'm already awake and there's a good deal to do in the house before dinnertime. Why don't you stay in bed and let me send you a little breakfast as soon as 'Aunt Rachel' has it ready? Then you can take your time about dressing and wandering around the house until time for Johnny and Belle to get here. Mamma and Papa want you to take it easy for a few days, but I know you aren't going to stay in that bed any longer than you have to. Here, let me help you with your wrapper and slippers. Then, after you've washed your face, you can tuck yourself back in bed for awhile."

Petite slipped her arms into the welcome woolen robe and wiggled her feet into the heavy crocheted slippers that Carrie held out for her. The room was quite cold, for the fire in the grate had burned itself out during the night and would have to be started anew when the colored folk came to work. She poured a little water from the pitcher into the bowl which Carrie, after using it, had carefully emptied into a large waste jar kept close by for that purpose. The water was cold as she splashed it on her eyes and face. It made her skin tingle and feel good and full of life. She dried her face and hands and ran a brush over the tangles in her curly hair. Then she jumped out of her slippers and quickly back into the warm bed.

Before long she heard Mamma and Papa stirring in their room. Farther back in the house, other happy sounds told her that Julia and the children were up and that preparations for breakfast were well under way. Thanksgiving Day was off to a good start!

Old Friends in the House

After her breakfast in bed, Petite got up to dress in a room now warm and comfortable from the fire that Julia had coaxed into bright existence. All the family had been in to wish her good morning, from tall, handsome Brother Jimmie to little Nootsie, whose mind had been too much occupied with thoughts of getting his "drits an' eggs" to pay much attention to anything else. Now they had all scattered to different parts of the house and grounds, and she was left alone.

She carefully looked over the dresses that Julia had unpacked and hung in the armoire and finally decided on her favorite "next to best" as the one she wanted to wear. It was a pretty, dark plaid with a solid vest-like front and matching cuffs of green velveteen, and two rows of gold buttons marching down the front. It was made much like the popular "walking dresses" worn by grown ladies, but differed in length from the adult styles since it stopped about twelve inches from the floor, thereby showing her black stockings and high-topped buttoned shoes. In a few years, when her dresses were longer, she would wear sheerer stockings, and her boots would have high heels. But then, too, she would have to wear her hair put-up and remember always to act like a lady. She was perfectly willing to wait.

Once dressed, she turned to the mirror and busied herself with combing her hair. It was cut short over her forehead where it lay in soft bangs. In the back she tied it with a dark ribbon and let the ends hang free. She wasn't exactly a beauty, she decided as she studied her reflection, but neither could she complain about her looks. Her round face, the slight upward tilt to her nose, and the large brown eyes that belonged

Sugar Petite

to both sides of her family, all gave her a happy, friendly look. She might never be as beautiful as Mamma and Sister Carrie, but she'd do all right . . . With a final glance, she turned her back on the mirror and left the room.

The wide entrance hall into which she stepped ran the entire depth of the house and from it a stairway led upward to the second floor. Her eyes flew immediately to the front door, which to her had always seemed one of the most wonderful parts of Belle Vale. It was a huge, double affair made of heavy panelled walnut. On either side and across the top, it was flanked by square panes of brightly colored imported glass which gave it a warm and somehow very festive appearance, whether viewed from within or without.

The children all loved these panes of glass, which seemed almost magic to them, not only because of the gorgeous and amazing colors imparted to the outside world, but because this was a one way treat. From the outside the glass was opaque, rendering the little viewers from within perfectly safe from having their stares returned. How often, when Papa was out on the gallery talking with a caller, the children had amused themselves with peeping through the small colored windows, their tiny noses flattened against the glass and gaily reflecting its rainbow colors. They had invented a special game consisting of muffled giggles and whispered singsong: "Oh, see Mr. *Red* Man; now he's Mr. *Green* Man; now he's Mr. *Yellow* Man, etc." that went on indefinitely, with small faces moving from one pane of glass to another.

Old Friends in the House

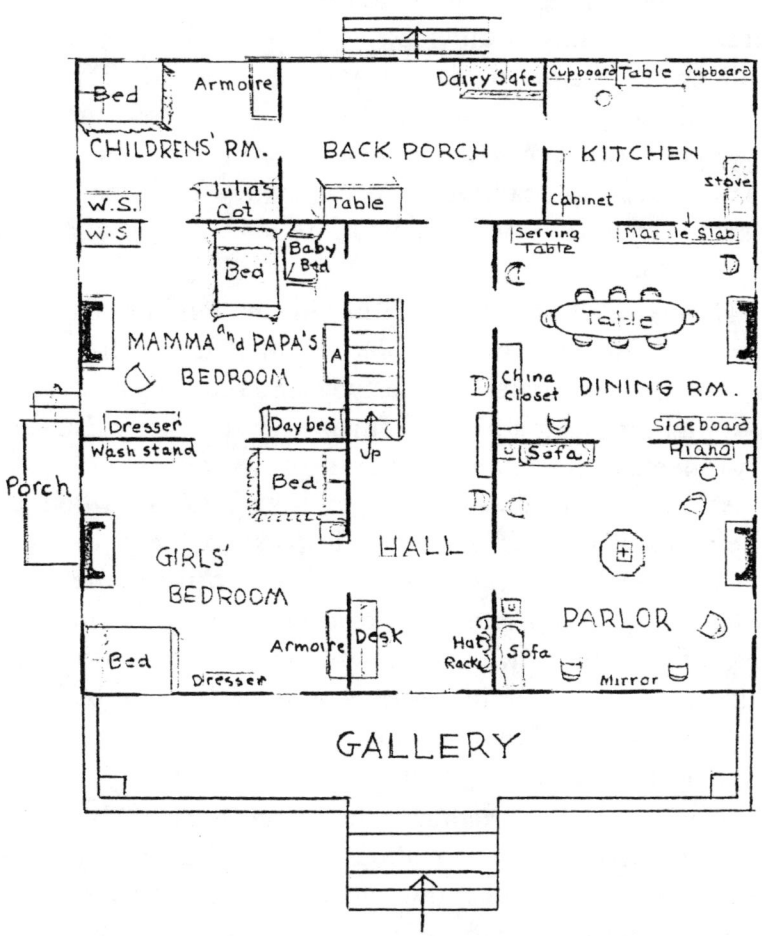

Belle Vale Downstairs Floor Plan

Sugar Petite

Of course, if Papa or his friend should become curious about the strange sounds coming faintly through the heavy door, they could look as hard as they might and still never be able to see a thing; and should they start toward the door, there was always plenty of time for scampering feet to make a hasty exit through one of the many openings leading from the hall. But Papa really never seemed to mind. At least, he never asked about it afterward.

However, there was one thing in the hall about which he did mind very much indeed, and that was his desk. It stood along the left wall as you entered the front door —a high, imposing piece of furniture with many drawers and pigeonholed compartments of various sizes. This was Papa's "business office," as he often explained to them. Each drawer and each little space held its own set of records—all the business of the entire plantation. That was why no one else was ever allowed to touch it, except Jimmie now that he was helping with the management of Belle Vale. Petite wondered how he had felt the first time Papa let him open one of the drawers. Her own hand trembled at the very thought.

She couldn't remember the time herself, but the family loved to tease her about once, when she was very tiny, when Papa had found reason to suspect that someone had been tampering with the papers in his desk. Now, sweet and gentle as her father usually was, he could be quite the opposite when he was really upset; and this time he was so angry that he had had everyone fairly quaking at the sound of his voice. Suddenly, so they told her, she had climbed down from Mamma's lap and

Old Friends in the House

started jumping up and down, clapping her little hands together and shouting, "Twarn't me, thank Gawd! Twarn't me!" Even Papa had stopped his storming to laugh as Mamma remarked sadly that her baby had been spending too much time with the colored folk.

She didn't know the end of the story—whether or not the real culprit was ever found—but looking now at the desk, she felt sure that nothing could have a more forbidding or unfriendly appearance. And yet, at the same time, she knew that, if necessary, she would be willing to protect it almost with her own life, so deeply had its importance been impressed upon her ever since she could remember.

Across the hall, just inside the front door, stood another piece of furniture, and this one looked as friendly as the desk did not. It was a hat rack—a large stand complete with hooks and mirrors mounted on a handsomely carved walnut back. The pattern of the carving contained many curves and scrolls which seemed to Petite to give it a very jovial look. She liked to think that it was smiling in a friendly way at all of Belle Vale's visitors. She could almost hear what it was trying to say: *"Do come in! We're so glad to have you! And please let me hold your hat and cane while you're visiting with us!"* Of course she never discussed with anyone how she felt about the hatrack, but even today she had the special feeling that it was smiling at her as if trying to welcome her home. She reached out her hand and gave it an affectionate pat as she walked past it into the parlor.

Her beautiful, beloved parlor! This had always been her favorite room, not only because it was the prettiest,

Sugar Petite

with its softly flowered, velvety carpet and dark red drapes, but because to her it had always seemed the very center of Belle Vale, as if it must have been there first, with all the rest—the house, the outbuildings, and even the fields—somehow placed around it.

No, more than that, she decided, it all seemed built around the mahogany, octagonal shaped table that stood in the exact center of the room, proudly holding the large family Bible—a beautiful book measuring nine by twelve inches, handsomely bound in brown, gold-tooled leather. She went over now and fondly turned the cover, pausing to look at the first of the familiar old pages, the frontispiece bearing the publisher's name and date. It was edited in England in 1826 and published by J. B. Lippincott Co., Philadelphia, in 1859. She counted off the years on her fingers. That was two years after Mamma and Papa were married, which made it twenty-seven years old. The Bible was one year younger than Brother Johnny and one year older than Belle. Already it was quite an old book. In addition to the two Testaments there were many pages of commentaries and references which she intended to read when she was older. Right now she preferred looking at the pictures—beautiful, full page engravings vividly illustrating different stories in the Bible.

The children were all familiar with the Bible stories and also with many hymns and prayers, for Mamma and Papa saw to it that this part of their life was not neglected although they were able to attend church only at infrequent intervals. They were Episcopalians, and whenever services were to be held by a visiting

Old Friends in the House

minister, as many of the family as were able would pile into the carriage and ride to the small white-framed building some five or six miles away at Devall. There they would always see many of their good friends in the community who also were members of that church, all lingering for a while after service to exchange greetings and bits of family news. The minister who included the little church in his round of mission visits often spent the night at Belle Vale. During the evening he would read to the family from the Bible and join them in singing hymns around the old piano in the corner of the room. The children loved his visits and looked forward to them with much eagerness. The Bible stories always seemed very real and heaven very close after he had been with them.

Petite glanced briefly at several of her favorite pictures and then, between the old and new Testaments, she sought out the pages devoted to family records. She smiled as she noted the entries. The first page was marked *Births* and already it was quite well filled, starting with the birthdates of her parents and ending with Nootsie's real name of William Abraham, with the date and hour of the various arrivals carefully noted in her father's flawless handwriting. On the pages devoted to *Marriages* there were only three entries—Mamma and Papa's, Brother Johnny's, and Sister Belle's. She cautiously lifted out a small dried bunch of pressed flowers—probably from Belle's bridal bouquet, she thought, as she held it in her hand for a moment before putting it back. There was also a page marked *Deaths* but it was empty . . . Very carefully she closed the book.

Sugar Petite

Yes, this was the way a home should be, with the Bible at its very heart. She wondered if Papa had ever thought of it that way. She must remember to ask him.

As she looked up, her glance was met by the dark eyes of Grandmother staring from her gold framed portrait on the wall just to the right of the marble mantel. Grandmother was pretty in a severe sort of way, with her regular features and dark coloring, but the unsmiling look in her eyes and the somber lace-trimmed gown she was wearing gave her a gloomy and uncomfortable look. Petite had never known her, and Mamma never mentioned her. Perhaps she had been as stern a mother as she appeared in her portrait. If you looked very closely, you could see a hole torn through the canvas at the base of her throat. When he was a very little boy, Brother Jimmie did this one day with a door key with which he was playing, and later he had rather proudly related how it happened. The portrait had been taken down, awaiting the repair of its picture cord, and was standing against the wall as he played about the room. She made him mad, he said, because everywhere he

Old Friends in the House

went, her dark eyes seemed to follow him, even after he had told her to stop! Petite often wondered, but never asked, why the damage was never repaired.

Across the room, in a similar heavy gold frame, hung a portrait of Great-Grandfather. It was even more frightening looking than the other, for Great-Grandfather was an ugly, redheaded gentleman with a scowling face and a drooping lower lip. How, thought Petite, could Mamma have happened in such a sullen looking family? — Mamma, who always seemed happy, and whose main interest in life was loving others and seeing that they were happy, too. Was it possible that her own childhood had been lacking in love and happiness? She sighed and shrugged her shoulders. There were some questions that were better left unasked.

And, after all, you didn't have to look at these portraits if you didn't want to. There was one other in the room, this one of Mamma's father, who was much more kindly looking than the others; and the rest of the room was pretty enough to make up for any shadow cast by gloomy appearing ancestors. The white marble mantel between the richly draped windows was delicately designed, the mantel shelf displaying a pair of handsome vases decorated with the forms of graceful maidens. The parlor set of two sofas and several matching chairs of carved mahogany was upholstered in black cambric over the harsh but fashionable horsehair interior. Mamma was very proud of her parlor furniture. Belle Vale might have seen hard times since the War, but in the gold framed mirror over the mantel the room was softly reflected with all the glory of its more prosperous years.

In the corner between the fireplace and the dining

Sugar Petite

room door stood a dainty little Playel piano with Papa's music rack placed beside it. All of the girls were given both piano and singing lessons as soon as they were old enough, so Papa and his flute never lacked accompaniment when the family settled down to an evening of music as they often did after supper. Petite lifted the keyboard cover and, seating herself on the round, fringed piano stool, played a few soft chords. She thought with a shudder of the story Mamma loved to tell about it. When the Yankees were shelling the shore from the river and Papa had made her leave Belle Vale to hide in a cabin back in the canebrakes, she had instructed the slaves to carry her little piano with her, along with her other dearest possessions. In their excitement they had dropped it in the bayou, where it stayed all of one watery night, but later Papa had had it restored to its original beauty and tone.

Suddenly she jumped up from the stool. She hadn't yet been to see the thing she loved most in all the house—Mamma's little girl portrait in the dining room!

The dining room was separated from the parlor by wide sliding doors. It was a large room with a center table that could be extended to seat as many as twenty people, and several side pieces of heavy furniture. From it one door opened into the hall and another into the kitchen. Over a marble-topped serving table there was also a "pass through" opening into the kitchen, through which "Aunt Rachel" handed her steaming triumphs for "Aunt Harriet" to serve to the family.

Today the table was already set in readiness for midday Thanksgiving dinner. It fairly shone with its white damask cloth and best family silver and china, with a bowl of fruit and magnolia leaves arranged in the center.

Old Friends in the House

Soon Papa would be seated at one end and Mamma at the other, with all their older children gathered between them, including the two new members whom marriage had added to the family in recent years. Their two younger children and two grandchildren would be fed by a colored nurse at the side table set in one corner of the room. There would be rich, dark gumbo; turkey with dressing and gravy; sweet potatoes and a variety of early winter vegetables from the garden; and for dessert, delicious ambrosia made of orange sections and freshly grated coconut, followed by black, black coffee served in tiny cups.

But to all of this Petite gave only a passing thought as she went to stand beneath the portrait hung between the two windows draped in gold. Here was Mamma as a little girl—a beruffled, white-dressed little girl with long, dark hair hanging about her shoulders and, on one round arm, a basket filled with spring flowers apparently plucked from the garden pictured in the background. Her face was sweet and delicate looking, and her large brown eyes seemed startlingly full of thought for one so young. Petite always felt like reaching up and trying to pull the little girl out of the frame to hug her to herself. But then she would remember that it was only her own Mamma, now grown and with her own family of children.

"What would you have thought," she silently asked the portrait, "if you could have known that someday you would own a plantation and have nine little children of your own? Would you have been afraid to grow up?"

"If I knew that I'd be scared to death," she decided about herself, and sank into the nearest chair, suddenly feeling very weak.

5. Papa

Thanksgiving dinner was over. It had been wonderful, every minute of it, until she had made a little fool of herself at the very end of the meal. And now here she was, back in bed, waiting for Papa to come in to talk with her. Petite gave the bedclothes an angry kick, then buried her head under the pillow as if trying to hide from herself. Of all the stupid people she had *ever* known, she was the worst—thirteen years old and still acting like a baby!

Everything about the dinner had been just right, clear through the last drop of coffee in the after dinner cups. "Aunt Rachel's" food was the very best yet, and it was wonderful having all of the family together again. Brother Johnny had sat at Mamma's right, with Belle in the place of honor beside Papa. Her parents had both looked so happy and proud of their big family that Petite had stolen a secret glance of admiration at *little girl Mamma* in the portrait looking down on them.

And then they had come to the end of the meal when, every year at Thanksgiving time, each member of the family told what had happened during the past year to make him the most thankful.

Papa had started it off by expressing thanks for the splendid cane year they had had, with the weather just right for one of the finest crops he could remember. Sister Lizzie, who was Brother Johnny's wife and was sitting at Papa's left, had told how grateful she was over her little daughter Josie's recent recovery from a serious sick spell. Next came Jimmie, who was thankful that he had successfully passed his courses at the University and could now help Papa with the plantation. Everyone had

Papa

clapped over this, for Jimmie had found going to college a tedious task and his graduation was regarded as quite a triumph by all the family.

And then it had been Petite's turn. She had started off, very calmly, to say what she had planned: "I'm more thankful than I've ever been for anything in my whole life to be . . . to be home again with my family!" And then, before even she herself realized what was happening, she had burst into tears.

Completely surprised, for a moment no one had said a word. Jimmie had quickly handed her his best linen handkerchief in which to hide her face and Eva, whose turn came next, had rolled her eyes in a panicky sort of way and blurted out, "Well, I'm awful thankful that Petite got sick!"

This was such a strange statement that everyone had laughed, including Petite herself, and the awkward situation had come to an end. She couldn't remember, however, what any of the other "thankfuls" were. She had been too embarrassed to pay any attention and, even without looking at him, she had felt Papa's eyes fixed on her in a very troubled way.

As they left the table to go into the parlor, he had held her back to tell her that he thought she'd had enough excitement for today and had better go back to bed for awhile. He would come in later to talk with her. She had wanted to tell him that really she felt all right, but his mouth was set in the firm line which always meant no arguing. So back to bed she had gone.

Petite had often tried to figure out just how she felt about Papa. It wasn't that she loved him more than Mamma; that could never be. Mamma, with her gentle ways, her pretty, low voice and soft, comforting hands,

Sugar Petite was the dearest thing in all the world. And yet, there was a special sort of closeness between her and her father that made it possible for her to talk with him almost as if she were talking with herself. He was so strong and steady and sure about everything, with a ready answer to every question and a solution for any problem that might arise. He could be very stern when occasion demanded it—with his family as well as with his colored folk—but under the hard exterior they all knew the bigness and gentleness of his heart.

"*He's just the way he looks,*" thought Petite, "*sort of short and square and strong looking, and his beard and straight-lined mouth give him kind of a gruff appearance —but when you look at his eyes, you know how kind he is. He's like a coconut,*" she decided with a smile, thinking of the sweet, milky fruit in the dinner dessert, "*hard and whiskery on the outside but all full of — is it the Bible that calls it the 'milk of human kindness'?*"

She snuggled deeper under the pillow over her head. She was having a good time with her little game of thought. But wouldn't Papa simply *die* if he knew she was comparing him with a coconut! This was one idea she had better keep to herself. No one else could ever understand just what she meant . . .

So engrossed was she with her secret meditations that she jumped when she felt someone gently pulling at the covers on her bed. She popped her head out from under the pillow and, sure enough, there was Papa, come to see her as he had promised. One look at his eyes and she knew that he wasn't going to scold her for breaking down in such an unladylike fashion at the dinner table. She held out her hands to him and moved over in bed to allow him room to sit beside her.

Papa

"I'm sorry," she said, going straight to the subject. "I don't know what made me act like that. All of a sudden, I was just crying—"

But Papa didn't even seem to hear her.

"Petite," he said, his voice sounding very serious, "I've been thinking a lot about you the last few days and I've reached a decision. You're not going back to school this year." Her heart gave a wild jump of joy. "Miss Valcourt will just have to fit your lessons in with the other children's here at home. Next year . . ." He paused and patted the hand he was holding. "Next year, you'll be fourteen, and then you should really be old enough to be away from home. Being homesick is nothing to feel ashamed about—it happens to anyone who has been part of a real family—but the break must come sometime, and it's harder for some people than for others."

"Oh, Papa!" Petite's heart was so full that for a moment she could say no more. Another year at Belle Vale as one of the children, instead of trying to be grown-up in a school away from home! Had anyone *ever* been happier than she was right now? But then she clung hard to his hand as the thought of the future pushed in again.

"But, Papa," she asked uncertainly, "how am I going to know if I'm old enough? I thought this year that I wanted to go with Lena. I thought I was old enough then, but I wasn't. I just couldn't *stand* it away from home! How can you tell, Papa? How do you know when you're grown-up and not a little girl any more?"

He put his hands over his face for a moment, but she knew that he wasn't laughing at her; just thinking how best to answer her question.

Sugar Petite

"Well," he said at last, "I suppose there are several ways you can know. Maybe, someday, you'll discover that people are leaning on you and depending on you for help, instead of just taking care of you as they do when you are a child. Maybe a difficult situation will arise and you'll find yourself handling it alone, as a grown person would. Then you'll know you're old enough to take care of yourself. Or maybe . . ." He hesitated and looked at her with a funny, new expression in his eyes. "Maybe a real attractive boy will come along, and you'll decide right then that you want to stop being a little girl and start thinking about grownup things."

"Oh, no!" protested Petite, "not that, Papa — not a boy!"

Her father smiled. "Well, then," he went on, "maybe you'll just discover one day that you're thinking like a grownup. You know, people who are mentally grown enjoy being quiet and alone sometimes—just alone with themselves and their own thoughts."

"But I do *now*," Petite exclaimed excitedly. "I like to think about things all by myself. Why, just now when you came into the room, that's what I was doing with the pillow on my head. I was having a wonderful time just with my own thoughts."

"Care to share them with me?" he asked.

Thinking of the coconut, she blushed a rosy pink as she shook her head.

Papa laughed. "I don't think we have a thing to worry about," he said. "I think our Sugar Petite is nearer to being a young lady than she wants to admit, even to herself."

He leaned over to kiss her very gently on the cheek.

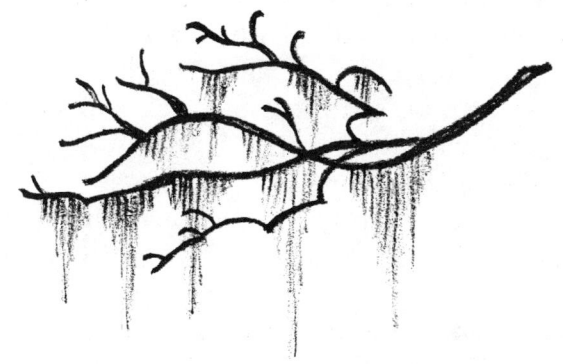

6. In the Tree House

"May I come up?"

Petite was standing at the foot of the big old pecan tree in the front yard, looking up into its branches, now bare and clearly revealing the strange wooden structure that the children called their "tree house."

She knew that her company wasn't wanted. Ever since Johnny and Jimmie had built the house many, many years ago, it had been a family rule that anyone who wanted to be alone simply pulled up the rope ladder which was the only means of ascent. It was pulled up now and there was no reply from above. But barely showing over the sides of the clumsily enclosed, box-like platform, she could see the top of Eva's curly head.

It was Sunday afternoon, just three days after Thanksgiving, but already Petite looked like a different child. The color had come back into her cheeks, and her dark eyes had regained the sparkle that was usually so much a part of them. If Papa had entertained any doubts about

Sugar Petite

his decision to let her remain at home, he had none now. He hadn't mentioned the matter again since their little talk together, but he smiled whenever he looked at her and saw how well and happy she seemed.

She picked up an old piece of brick and knocked politely on the bark of the tree.

"Eva, may I *please* come up?"

Still there was no reply, and the top of the head all but disappeared as its owner crouched lower in an effort not to be seen.

Eva had been avoiding her ever since her first day at home, not only by making herself absent as often as possible but also by lowering her eyes and keeping a miserable silence whenever they happened to be together. It worried Petite. She knew that her little sister loved her and wanted her to be at home; her funny but well meant remark at the dinner table had shown that. No, Eva was upset and uncomfortable about something, probably still about her face, and this was just the chance she'd been waiting for to talk with her alone and try to straighten things out.

"Eva—" her voice grew more insistent. "I *know* you're up there, and I want to talk to you." Still nothing but silence above.

"If you let me come up," she persisted, desperately turning once more to the old trick of holding out a bribe, "I was going to tell you an awfully scary ghost story that's really supposed to have happened in New Orleans a few years ago."

There was a slight, undecided rustle inside the tree house, followed by Eva's red face appearing over the edge. The next instant the end of the ladder came hurtling down to the ground below.

In the Tree House

It took Petite only a few seconds to climb up the rope rungs and over the side of the house. She gathered up her awkward skirt in a rather unladylike manner as she climbed, but no one was watching and she straightened it out as best she could as she seated herself opposite her little sister. There really wasn't enough room up here for two people unless they were very small ones indeed. Her tree house days were just about over she decided, as she sat with pulled up knees, her feet tucked as much as possible out of Eva's way. Eva was sitting with her back against one side of the house and, partly hidden behind her, Petite could see a small box with the remains of a bar of "Johnny Crook" which she had been eating when interrupted. She really needn't have tried to hide it. There was enough of the sweet molasses and coconut confection left on her face to show what she'd been doing. Anyway, Petite certainly wouldn't have asked for any, uninvited guest that she was.

"Tell me the story," said Eva after a moment of strained silence.

"Well, I'll tell you," replied Petite, "but don't you tell anyone else. I don't think Papa would approve of it. It's something that was written up in the newspaper about four years ago. One of the girls at school found the clipping hidden in her mother's desk, and she brought it to school to us—only, of course, the teachers didn't know about it."

"That was very naughty of her," said Eva righteously, "taking it without telling her mother."

"I know, but of course I looked at it, too, because all the others did. Only now I'm sort of sorry I did, because it was so scary!"

"Go on, tell me about it."

Sugar Petite

"Well, it seems that in the old Parish Prison down there, all the prisoners in a certain cell started trying to commit suicide and lots of them really did. And the ones who lived to tell about it all told the same story about a beautiful, red-headed woman who would suddenly appear and smile at them and then start torturing them so bad that all they could do was want to kill themselves."

"Mercy sakes!" exclaimed Eva. "What did she do to them?"

"It didn't say. I guess she stuck pins in them and things like that. Well, anyway, they stopped using that cell. After a while she began appearing in another cell on the same floor, and six more prisoners killed themselves. Several policemen saw her, too, and they named her "The Redheaded Countess" because she had such gorgeous, long red hair and walked sort of like a queen."

"And then what?"

"Well, that's about all it said, except that once one of the officers passed her on the stairs, and she touched him—and you know what?"

"What?"

"Her fingers burned a hole right through his coat and scorched his skin. He said so himself."

"Oh, my goodness! Do you suppose that, being such a wicked ghost, she might have come straight from *You Know Where*, and that's why she was so hot?"

"Maybe so," said Petite, "but of course none of it really happened. You know Papa says there aren't *really* any ghosts . . . Still, seeing it in the newspaper did make it *look* awfully real."

The story had worked. Eva's eyes were bright with excitement and she had forgotten all about being em-

In the Tree House

barrassed in her sister's presence. But all this was really getting nowhere.

"Your face looks a lot better," Petite said, deciding to waste no more time in getting to the subject.

Sure enough, Eva immediately lowered her eyes, and the color in her face deepened a shade as she struggled within herself trying to determine how to answer. At length she took a long, miserable breath and blurted out: "I told you a lie, Petite. I didn't sunburn it at all . . ." She paused, not knowing how to go on with her confession.

Petite hurried to help her out. "I know it. I've known it all along," she said, "and you really didn't tell the lie; I did. Julia told me all about that awful fruit peddler and his selling you the cream for your face, and I just made it up about the sunburn because I . . . well, I thought you might not want me to know."

A look of relief flooded Eva's face; then her eyes suddenly filled with tears. "Oh, Petite," she wailed, "I'm so awfully bad. I do things behind people's backs and then I tell stories and . . . and I'm so *selfish!*" She reached behind her and pulled out the box of sticky candy. "I didn't even want you to have any of my 'Johnny Crook'." Then, before Petite could say anything to comfort her, she began to cry. "I'm a—afraid," she sobbed. "I just know if I'd die I couldn't get into heaven!"

This was more than Petite had bargained for. She hunched herself across the rough floor until she was sitting close enough to her little sister to put an arm around her. "Now you stop crying this instant," she ordered gently, "and listen to me. I . . . I've thought it all over lots of times, and I'll tell you just what I think about getting into heaven."

Sugar Petite

Eva's tears stopped as suddenly as they had started, as she drew a slightly grimy sleeve across her eyes and waited. Petite leaned her head against the wooden back and closed her eyes in an effort to concentrate on what she was going to say. It would be hard putting into words the rather hazy ideas she had worked out for herself about the blessed hereafter.

"Well, it's like this," she started slowly. "I think that up in heaven the big *Book of Names* St. Peter keeps must be divided into two parts. One half is for grown-ups and the other half for children. In the children's part I think maybe the page for each name is marked with a line drawn down the middle . . ." She paused to draw an imaginary line in the air. "On one side St. Peter writes the bad thing that's done, and on the other side the reason—'cause children usually *do* have a reason for doing bad things. Maybe it would say, 'Told a lie' and the reason: 'Afraid he would be punished'; or 'Pulled the puppy's tail and the reason: 'Because he didn't know that it hurt'; or 'Stole some cookies out of the kitchen *because* he was so hungry', or even 'Bought face cream when she knew she shouldn't *because* she wanted so much not to have freckles.'" She heard Eva give a broken sigh. "I think God understands all about children," she went on, "and that's why I think He almost always lets them into heaven.

"Now with grownups it's different. By the time you're grown, you're supposed to know just what's right and what's wrong, and that you're not supposed to do the wrong thing for *any* reason. That's why on a grownup's page in the *Book of Names* I don't think there's any place for excuses. If you do something bad when you're

In the Tree House

grown, it's just done, that's all; and St. Peter doesn't care why."

She opened her eyes and looked at Eva, whose face was a picture of wide-eyed enchantment. "That's one reason why I'm in no hurry to grow up," she said. "I'd much rather just stay in the children's part of the *Book* and I know I can forget once in a while to be perfect, and still have it understood."

Eva nodded her head in approval. This was a new and very comforting idea.

"But I don't think God always understood so well about children," said Petite. "It was only after He'd come down to earth and been one Himself that He really knew how hard it is to be good." She stopped to think a minute before going on. She was beginning to enjoy her own little sermon. "You know, His coming down on earth changed lots of things. Before He came people weren't supposed to eat certain foods like ham and crabs and shrimp; but after that, He decided it was all right . . ."

"I bet He never knew before how good they were," interrupted Eva. "I bet when He first tasted river shrimp, He decided people just oughta eat 'em!"

"Well, I don't know about that," Petite hastened to say, realizing that the subject was beginning to get a little out of hand. Furthermore, a sudden, startling picture had flashed across her mind and it didn't seem at all right—an otherwise typical meal in Bible times including a huge platter of iced river shrimp which a number of saintly looking gentlemen were all solemnly peeling. Their long, loose sleeves kept getting in the way, while hovering in the background she imagined a little white-

Sugar Petite

clad angel busily passing around a great towel on which to wipe their juicy fingers. She blinked her eyes and shook her head to rid herself of the picture.

"I never heard of river shrimp in the Bible," she said firmly. "Papa says that Louisiana is about the only place in the world where they're found . . ."

At that moment she was relieved to hear Carrie calling to them from below.

7. *Pinkie*

" 'Aunt Rachel,' what's the matter with Pinkie? He doesn't want to talk to me any more."

Petite perched herself on the tall, three-legged stool in the kitchen, close beside the table where "Aunt Rachel" was busily rolling out pastry for a pie. It was going to be one of her wonderful pecan pies, and the rich molasses filling was already cooked and waiting in a saucepan on the big, black stove.

Usually Mamma didn't allow the children to visit with the colored folk while they were busy, for it kept them from their work; but with "Aunt Rachel" it was different. She could work and talk at the same time, her strong black fingers never pausing an instant at whatever task they were performing. She had been with the family ever since Petite could remember, and cooking seemed as much a part of her as her smiling black face or the neat cotton dress, checked apron and bright head-kerchief she always wore.

It was an early December Saturday morning, and through the window behind the table Petite could look into the sun-filled back yard. The other children had gone back to the stable to ride "Old Jim," and the house seemed wonderfully quiet and peaceful without them. She had somehow forgotten, while in New Orleans, how noisy children could be. And yet, she reminded herself, it was good to be one of them again.

She was completely back in the routine of living at home. Five days of every week she attended classes under the instruction of Miss Valcourt, the governess who lived

Sugar Petite

with them during the school year, occupying the large Guest Room upstairs. Classes were held across the hall in the Boys' Room, which was also used as a class room during the school months, with a desk for the governess and chairs for her young pupils. Petite and Eva were the only children in the family who were of school age right now, but there were five children from neighborhood families whose fathers brought them each morning before time for school to "take in" at nine o'clock and called for them again at three. During the noon hour, the governess and family ate dinner downstairs. The other children brought their lunches with them.

Petite liked Miss Valcourt and knew that Papa felt very fortunate to have found her for them. Her real home was in New Orleans where she had a French father and an English mother, and Papa considered it quite an advantage that she spoke both languages fluently. He, too, had spoken French as a child, although he had completely abandoned it as a speaking language after going away to college.

Miss Valcourt had started teaching the children a little French in addition to the regular subjects of reading, writing, arithmetic, spelling, history and geography; and Petite was finding it a lot of fun learning new words for everything around her. In fact, Miss Valcourt had a way of combining fun with everything she taught, an approach which was quite different from some of the other governesses they had had. Especially was this true at piano lesson time when she used a delightful method of instruction all her own. Papa always made sure that the children's governess could teach music as well as the regular studies, and each little girl was given three piano lessons a week after school. This meant that someone had to get

Pinkie

up early enough to do her practicing before breakfast every morning. But that was working out fine, too, for Petite liked to get it over with before the day really started, while Eva said that she'd rather sleep a little later, even if it meant taking time away from her play after school was out.

"What's de mattah wif Pinkie?" "Aunt Rachel" repeated as she cut out a large round of thinly rolled dough and, after skillfully turning it into the pie pan, began trimming off the edge. "Well, dat's sumpin' Ah don't rightly know mahself—" She looked up and shook her head as her fingers fluted the pastry around the rim of the pan. "He ain't ezzactly ben hisself fo' some time now—dat is, ef you can say po' Pinkie has ever ben hisself!"

"I know," said Petite gently, her heart suddenly feeling very warm and full at the thought of the poor old colored man. She had asked Papa all about him—what made him so different from everyone else, with his funny pinkish skin, his white hair and pale, weak eyes that never stayed still. Papa had told her that he was an *albino,* and had explained a little about what that meant. "But he doesn't even act the way he used to. You know, 'Aunt Rachel,' he'd always talk to *me,* even when he wouldn't talk to anybody else. But since I've been home, he just barely speaks, without even looking at me. Do you s'pose maybe he's sick or something?"

"Might be," agreed "Aunt Rachel." " 'Course Pinkie has always stayed to hisself; but all de years he's lived wif me an' Steve in our cabin, he ain't never ben as stan'-offish as now. At fust Ah thought he's jes' all grieved up over you goin' off to school; but now you's back, Ah do declare he seem worse 'n ever . . . Tell you what Ah

Sugar Petite

really thinks, ef you promise not to tell a soul—Ah thinks dem li'l Triplett debbils has got him worried sick!"

"The Tripletts?" asked Petite. She looked out of the window in the direction of the servants' house in the back yard where Will and Lou Triplett lived with their three little boys. Will tended the horses, pigs, and the few cows that were kept for milk for the family, and was also general handyman for the whole backyard, while "Aunt Lou" did the washing and ironing for the white family. Petite had known Jeff and Billy and Alec ever since they were born. Sometimes they were allowed to play with the white children, and they were always on hand to help pick up pecans in the fall. She had always thought they were cute little colored boys. Often they were naughty, she knew, but she had never thought of them as "li'l debbils."

"Ah don' know what dey's tole him," "Aunt Rachel" went on, "but Ah do know dey calls him names an' hollers things at him to tease him. Ah reckon dey's jes' now got ole enough to notice his looks. Ah stahted to say sumpin' to dere Maw, but Steve tell me: 'Stay off—no use stahtin' no fight on de place.'" She pushed her finished pie into the oven and slammed the heavy door rather **harder than necessary.**

"Well, I'll be!" exclaimed Petite as she hopped down from the stool. "Those horrid little boys! I just think I'll go look for Pinkie and *make* him talk to me. I'll find out for myself what's worrying him."

"In de veg'table gahden," volunteered "Aunt Rachel" helpfully, and added in a half-whisper: "God bless you, honey-chile!"

Pinkie

Petite walked slowly. She was in no hurry, partly because she wasn't sure just what she was going to say to Pinkie if she found him, and partly because it was too pretty a day to hurry about anything. The sun was soft and warm, as it often is in Louisiana wintertime. It felt more like springtime than a December day.

She passed the old kitchen building, now used as a storeroom since Papa had had the new kitchen added to the back of the house. In the old building the cooking had been done in a big fireplace with an oven built in the brick chimney-wall, an arrangement which always imposed a danger of fire should anything go wrong. Petite knew that that was why the kitchens in the older homes were always separate buildings back of the main house. But now, with its big iron stove, its cupboards and roomy cabinets, Belle Vale's new kitchen was quite the last word in safety and modern improvements. At the same time it was built, Papa had added the "Children's Room" at the back of the house, with storage space underneath; and also the large back porch where the daily supply of milk, cream and butter was kept fresh in a screened in "dairy safe," with ice delivered by boat from New Orleans several times a week.

Past the well with its accompanying dairy house and bathhouse, and past the corner of the chicken yard where she stopped a few minutes to watch the plump, well-fed chickens scratching in the soft dirt, she came at last to the gate leading through the fence to the vegetable garden.

Once on the other side, since this was really his domain, she began once again to think about Pinkie. Ever since she was a tiny little girl, she and the strange looking colored man had been the closest of friends. Mamma said

Sugar Petite

that she had loved him even when she was a baby, and this affection was returned with pitiful devotion by the poor love-starved old man. It was he who had first called her "Petite," which meant "little girl" in French and was the name she loved so dearly.

Most people thought that Pinkie was stupid because he was very shy and hardly ever spoke a word, but Petite knew that this wasn't so. He had always talked with her, and perhaps no one else in the world knew how much thinking really did go on back of those pale, dancing eyes. Of course, she had to admit that she didn't agree with much that he thought. Indeed, if Papa knew about it, he would doubtless disapprove of her talking with him at all, for the old man was a perfect storehouse of strange beliefs on almost every subject. Not only did he believe in ghosts, of which he could tell many tales of first hand experiences, but everything he did was in accordance with some peculiar set of rules.

Petite didn't object to his ideas about the weather and how to plant things. From him she had learned that if you killed a snake or a cat, it would rain; that if a bullbat swooped down low and said "broke," you could be sure that winter was over; and that you must never plant corn until the dogwood was in full bloom. She knew that everything that matured under the ground, like potatoes and carrots and beets, should be planted in the dark of the moon; but that those maturing on top, like beans and peas and squash, should be planted when the moon was full. Also that vegetable and melon seeds should always be sown by children so they would grow as the children grew; and that if, when a crop was planted, there should happen to be a woman nearby holding a flower in her hand, the harvest would be poor.

Pinkie

None of this seemed so bad. It was regarding the matter of ghosts and signs of good and bad luck that she wasn't so sure. Especially when he talked about sickness and dreams and death, she sometimes felt a little guilty about listening to him at all. The good dreams seemed all right—trees and horses and churches and clear water all meant good luck, and talking about them didn't worry her at all. But when he talked about dreams of pulling a tooth meaning death was coming, just the same as if you heard an owl close to the house or a dog howling at night, she didn't like the feeling it gave her.

Then there were all his queer charms and cures for different kinds of trouble, like a string of beads tied with nine knots fastened around your neck to cure a headache, and a garlic bag tied to your thumb to get rid of an aching tooth. Occasionally she tried to argue with him about some of these things, but he wouldn't listen to her. He said maybe the charms didn't work for white folks but they did for "cullud" folks, just the same as "cullud" folks could see ghosts better than white folks could. However, disapprove though she might, Petite never grew tired of listening to him, which was the main reason now for her concern over his acting so strange and withdrawn.

She didn't find him in the vegetable garden as she had expected, so she wandered on back, past the grape arbor, to the orchard, thinking that it would be harder to see him back there where some of the old fruit trees were quite large. He was there, however, and almost immediately she saw him lying under a pear tree, his back propped against its trunk and a battered old hat pulled down over his eyes.

Sugar Petite

"Pinkie!" She almost whispered his name.

At the sound of her voice the old man scrambled to his feet and pulled off his hat, which he silently turned over and over in his gnarled, pink hands as he stood before her.

"I didn't know if you were asleep."

He shook his head but didn't speak, his eyes steadfastly looking at the ground.

"Pinkie, what's the matter with you?" Petite asked abruptly. "I've tried to talk to you every time I've seen you since I've been back, and you never say a word. Are you sick . . . or are you just sorry I'm home?"

At the last question the old man looked up. For a moment he tried to fix his eyes on her, and in that instant she realized that they were full of tears. "Oh, no, ma'am . . . no, ma'am," he muttered brokenly. "Not sorry you's home, Lawd knows! It's jes' dat . . . dat . . . oh, don' talk to me, Petite, less de debbil git you!"

"The devil?" gasped Petite, hardly able to believe her ears. "The devil will get me if I talk to you? Now, Pinkie, where'd you ever get an idea like that?" And then as he stood miserably saying nothing, suddenly she knew. "The Triplett boys! Did Jeff and Billy and Alex tell you that?"

Pinkie nodded sadly. "Dey say dere Maw tell 'em dat's how come Ah looks so diffunt. 'Cause de debbil's in me, an' he'll git in anybody else dat talks to me. Dey jumps up an' down an' hollers at me: 'Debbil's got Pinkie! Don't talk to Pinkie!' Oh, Petite, maybe dey's right. Maybe dat *is* how come Ah looks de way Ah does."

"They just made it up," Petite declared angrily. "I don't believe their mother ever told them that!" Then

Pinkie

she asked gently: "Pinkie, didn't anyone ever tell you what makes you look different from other people?"

He shook his head. All his life he had stood apart, not knowing why he was unlike any other person he had ever seen. Petite struggled to remember what Papa had told her.

"It's because you're an *albino*," she said kindly, feeling sure of that much at least. "And that's just a word that means you don't have as much color in you as other people. Papa says that sometimes there are albino animals, like white mice, and sometimes there are albino birds. And you just happen to be an albino person, that's all. It has something to do with a thing in you called 'pigment.' Colored people have more of it than white people, and you don't have even that much."

Pinkie hadn't seemed able to grasp the first part of what she was saying; but as she pronounced the word *pigment,* he suddenly jumped to attention. "What dat word you say again?" he asked excitedly. "Pig—pig— what?"

"Pig-ment," repeated Petite slowly. "It's something most people have more of than you do."

The old face broke into a delighted grin. *"Pig-men,"* he murmured happily. "Well, Ah do declare! All de darkies is mo' pig-men dan me, an' all de white folks, too. Ole Pinkie, he's de leas' pig-man of 'em all! Thank you, Petite, thank you fo' tellin' me dis . . . an' if yo' pa say so, it mus' be true." He began chuckling to himself, something she had never known him to do before. "Jes' you wait 'til Ah see dem l'il rascals. Debbil, dey say! An' dem jes' mo' pig-men dan me!"

Petite was horrified. This wasn't what she had intended

Sugar Petite

to tell him at all! She opened her mouth to try to explain, and then suddenly closed it again. She would leave things just as they were. She had made Pinkie happy. For the first time in his poor old life he was feeling that he was better than any one else. If he had misunderstood what she said, she couldn't help it and she didn't care. As a matter of fact, she realized that she was very glad.

"Now, don't you worry any more," she said. "Anyhow, I've always liked you just as you are. I wouldn't want you any other way."

She left him still standing under the pear tree, chuckling to himself.

8. The Sugar Bowl Game

"Knit two, purl two; knit two, purl two." Petite sang the words to herself, her whole body swaying in rhythm as her fingers cautiously maneuvered the yarn from one needle to the other.

She had almost finished the wool shawl she was knitting as a Christmas surprise for Mamma. It was her first piece of knitting, started in New Orleans under Aunt Lydia's instruction; and since she'd been at home, Miss Valcourt had been helping her with it. The yarn was a beautiful shade of soft rosy-red and, in spite of a few bumpy places where the stitches hadn't acted just right, she was very proud of it and knew that Mamma was going to love it. Mamma hadn't been feeling very well lately, and Petite liked to think, as she worked, how nice and warm the shawl would keep her shoulders on cold days when the heat from the fireplaces wasn't quite enough for the big old rooms.

It was rather cold now in the Guest Room where she was sitting with the door closed in order that she might

Sugar Petite

work in secrecy. The room hadn't been used for several days because Miss Valcourt had gone home to spend the holidays with her family, and although today there was a fire in the hearth, it had not yet taken all the chill out of the high-ceilinged room. It was raining, and the patter of the drops on the roof made a lonesome sound. She wished Miss Valcourt could be with her now. They had enjoyed such good times together, knitting here in secret. Sometimes they had sung little French songs while she worked; sometimes Miss Valcourt had talked about her large family and their life together in New Orleans; and once she had told her about a vacation trip to France to visit a cousin of her father's—a wonderful adventure that had sounded like a make-believe story out of a book.

Today the room was very quiet, shut off from the rest of the house. It was the prettiest of all the bedrooms, with a handsome hand-carved set of rosewood furniture, a high four-poster bed with a tester of blue, a dresser and marble topped washstand, and a matching armoire. On one side of the fireplace was a window. On the opposite side, a door opened onto a small wooden-railed balcony overlooking the garden. The Boys' Room, across the hall, was its exact duplicate in plan but was furnished with practical, heavy oak furniture instead of the more feminine pieces in here.

Tonight Lena would sleep in this room with the friend she was bringing home from school with her. Petite felt again the pang of jealousy that had stabbed her the day Lena's letter arrived, asking if she might invite her classmate to visit them. She wanted Lena to herself, not up here in the Guest Room with a strange girl she had never met. But Mamma had sent permission at once, so she was trying to be enthusiastic, too. Lena's

The Sugar Bowl Game

letter said that her friend was a new-comer to Louisiana and that she had never been on a sugar plantation. It would be fun showing her around . . .

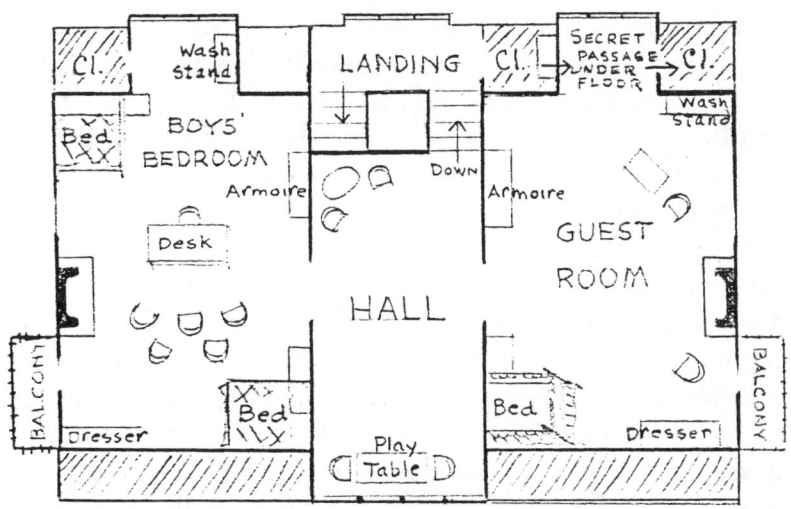

Carrie had gone to New Orleans with Papa to help him with his winter shopping and to bring the girls back to Belle Vale. Usually Mamma went with him each December, but this year she said she just didn't feel up to it. Petite wondered what they would bring back with them. It was so much fun welcoming Papa home after one of his trips, of which he took four or five each year in order to shop for supplies for the family and the plantation. Always, before he left, there was much excitement over the long list to be composed from which he was to do his buying. The children who needed new shoes were lined up in a row while he traced around their feet on a big piece of paper carefully marked with each name and the type of shoe that was needed. Petite

Sugar Petite

thought there was no other feeling in the world quite like the exciting, "tickley" feeling of having her feet traced for a new pair of shoes. It started at her toes, went straight up her back, and came out the top of her head.

When he returned after two or three days in the big city, everyone would gather around to see what he would unload from the wagon that had met him at the boat landing. In addition to the new shoes, there would be medicines and city food, dress materials and perhaps a new piece of furniture, a lamp, or some cooking utensils for "Aunt Rachel" to use in the kitchen. There would be a new book and new music for the piano, and always a surprise or two—a delightful New Orleans cake or confection, or some little piece of luxury that he hadn't been able to resist buying for Mamma. And in December there were what the children called the "mystery packages," one for each, which were quickly spirited away with not so much as a hint as to their contents, not to be seen again until Christmas morning . . .

A sudden knocking in the hall interrupted Petite's thoughts and sent her flying to hide her knitting under a pillow. But when she opened the door, she found that it wasn't Mamma after all. Instead, there stood Indie, Eva, Bena, and Nootsie, all lined up like a row of soldiers. Her heart gave a woeful bump as she sensed the end of her peaceful afternoon of knitting.

"Please, Petite," begged Eva, "will you come play with us?"

"Oh, Eva," she protested, "I'm doing something very important. Can't you play with Indie?"

"But it's raining, and we've played everything we can, indoors. We've played 'William Come Trimmle Toe' and 'All Round the Rose Bush' and 'Chickama,

The Sugar Bowl Game

Chickama, Craney-crow,'* and now we want to play the sugar bowl game."

"Well, go play it," said Petite, welcoming the thought of any game that would get them out of the way right then.

"But we don't have enough people. I'm going to be Papa, and Bena can be Aunt Lydia, and Nootsie can be the slave, and Indie the Yankee soldier . . ."

"Ah don' *want* to be no Yankee soldier!" exploded Indie.

"Well you *have* to be," insisted Eva, stamping her foot. "Nootsie has to be the slave 'cause he can't talk good enough to be anybody else, and you have to be the Yankee soldier 'cause there's nobody else for you to be 'cept Mamma, and you sure don't look like *her!*"

Indie rolled her big eyes, her buckteeth flashing in disapproval as she shook her head. "Don' want to be *no* Yankee," she repeated staunchly.

Eva was exasperated. "Now look here, Indie. I think that's downright ungrateful of you. Here the Yankees went to all that trouble to come way down here and free you from bein' a slave, and you don't even want to be one of 'em in a game. I just wish they could hear about it. I bet they'd want to come right back and unfree you again!"

Indie's position was shaken. "Well, awright," she whined. "Reckon Ah'll be a Yankee dis once, but Ah sho' nuff don' like dis game no how!"

Petite sighed. The easiest thing would be to get it over with and hope to return to her knitting. "All right,"

---

* See "Songs and Games from Belle Vale," *pages 170-180.*

Sugar Petite

she agreed, "I'll play it once if you'll leave me alone after that."

The game they were about to play was a favorite one with the children, its chief charm lying in the fact that it was the reenactment of an actual bit of family history. During the War Between the States, Papa had served as a secret agent to carry supplies and medicines behind the Confederate lines. The story about how the Yankees almost caught him had been told and retold until every word of it was known by heart. The next step, acting it out as a little play, had been a natural and fascinating development.

"We have everything all ready," announced Eva. Then she added pleadingly: "You don't mind if we use your tea set, do you, Petite?"

Petite looked at the little play table set before the large dormer window in the front part of the hall. It was carefully laid with the set of toy china which had been her Christmas present several years before. She could still remember the thrill of opening the package and finding the dainty handpainted china lying in its red velvet-lined box.

"Oh, Eva, you shouldn't have taken it without asking!"

"Well, I couldn't find you and, anyway, you're too big to play with it now."

Petite started to say that she was saving it for her own little girl to have someday; but seeing the longing look on her little sister's face, she softened her tone. "Well, all right for this time, but after this you must ask me first. Indie," she instructed, entering in spite of herself into the spirit of the game, "you and Nootsie go downstairs, and you send him up when we thump on the floor."

The Sugar Bowl Game

She, Eva and Bena arranged themselves around the table, which was set with three cups and saucers, the cream pitcher and sugar bowl in the center. There were only two chairs so Eva, who was being *Papa*, seated herself on the floor, politely leaving the chairs for the "ladies."

Petite, as *Mamma*, opened the conversation: "I'm so glad you could come home, dear, for a little visit with us. I've been so worried about you."

Papa (Eva): "Well, I'm glad, too. I'm pretty tired, you know, with all this riding back and forth and the Yankees everywhere. How are the children?"

Mamma: "Oh, they're fine. But Johnny has had a little cold" (at this point it was always fun to improvise with family news) "and baby Belle has a new tooth."

Papa: "My, my! Well, I'm glad sister Lydia can be here for a visit with you so's she can help out."

Aunt Lydia (Bena): "I'm glad, too. Want some coffee?"

Mamma: "*(Wait, Bena, I'm supposed to say that!)* Let's all drink a little coffee, dear, and then you can take a rest before you start back to the lines." She pretended to pour coffee into the three little cups, at the same time thumping on the floor with her foot as a signal to those below.

There was a patter on the steps and up trotted little Nootsie, who was supposed to be a slave bearing important news. At the head of the stairs, however, his mind suddenly went blank and he stood, finger in mouth, staring at the group around the table.

"Say: 'The Yankees are coming!'" whispered Petite.

"Yankees a-tummin'! Yankees a-tummin'!" screamed

Sugar Petite

Nootsie, hopping up and down, his small arms flapping like wings.

"Oh, dear," cried *Mamma*, as she jumped up from the table and threw her arms around *Papa*. "Whatever shall we do? Oh, I know—the secret passage, of course! Come, dear, quickly. Lydia, hide his coffee cup!"

While *Aunt Lydia* swiftly removed the cup and hid it behind the window drapes, *Mamma* hurried *Papa* to the door of a closet at the head of the stairs. This closet contained Belle Vale's only real secret, though no longer a carefully guarded one since the story of Papa's escape had spread quite widely over the neighborhood. Concealed by an old chest pushed against its back wall was the entrance to a passage way leading under the floor and emerging in the closet to the Guest Room. No one knew just what its original purpose had been. It was already part of the house when Grandfather gave Mamma the plantation as a wedding present; but, as far as they knew, only on this occasion of the Yankees' visit had it ever been put to any real use.

Petite and Bena now pulled the chest away from the entrance, and Eva took her place inside the passage, allowing them once more to push it into place. Petite couldn't imagine why Eva always wanted to be *Papa* in the game. It was dark and spooky in there and she didn't like it at all, but Eva seemed to think it was a lot of fun.

"Indie," Petite called down the stairs. "Time for the Yankees!"

Up the steps trudged unwilling Indie, dragging her feet and obviously begrudging her role. She knocked loudly on the newel post.

"Yes?" said *Mamma* sweetly, going to the make-believe

The Sugar Bowl Game

door. Then she drew back with a dramatic gasp of feigned surprise as she saw who stood without.

"Ah is de Yankee Ahmy!" announced Indie. "Ah done seed a hoss hitched outside an' Ah done come to fetch yo' husban'."

Petite smothered a giggle as she tried to regain the composure *Mamma* was supposed to show. Indie as a Yankee was just *too* ridiculous in every way! "Oh, do come in, sir," she said graciously, "but you are mistaken about my husband. He hasn't been here for several weeks."

"Ah done seed his hoss," insisted Indie, planting herself firmly on her huge feet and glaring at Petite with all the ferocity she imagined in a Yankee officer.

"Oh, you must mean the horse at the back door," said *Mamma*. "One of the colored boys rode on an errand for me to a neighboring place and has just returned."

"Don' look dat way to me. Gotta sarch de house, dat's what Ah gotta do!"

"Why of course, if you like. You may look anywhere you please, but you'll see that you're wrong. You won't find him here."

Mamma led the *Yankee Army* into the hall, where a thorough search was begun, with Indie crawling on her hands and knees to look under the table and in all the corners. *Mamma* stood with hands calmly folded, while *Aunt Lydia* and the diminutive *slave* looked on in unconcealed delight. Finally Indie placed herself in front of the hall closet, her hand upon the door knob. "How 'bout dis closet? Dis look like a good hidin' place!"

This was the most exciting part of the game, and it was fortunate that the *Army* didn't look just then at *Aunt*

Sugar Petite

Lydia and *the slave,* who were unable to resist jumping up and down in their enthusiasm.

"Well, look if you like," said *Mamma* placidly, "but you're just wasting your time."

"Yankee Ahmy's got plenty a time!" declared Indie sharply, giving vent to a bit of impudence she would never dare show before a white person in real life. She poked her head in the closet and peered around in the half darkness. "Don't see nothin' in here," she announced. "Reckon he couldn't squeeze hisself in none a dem drawers to de ole chest. Reckon you's right, lady. He ain't no whar ter be foun'!"

Mamma smiled. "If you had listened to me, you would have saved yourself a lot of trouble," she said. "But really, you've been very nice. My sister and I were just sitting down to a cup of coffee. Won't you join us?"

"Don' mind ef Ah do," accepted the *Yankee Army,* folding up her large frame beside the little table, while *Mamma* and *Aunt Lydia* gracefully seated themselves on the chairs. The *slave* immediately climbed in the *Army's* lap, but everyone pretended not to notice.

Mamma poured the imaginary coffee, *Aunt Lydia* having conveniently retrieved the cup from behind the drapes, and as she did so she said chidingly: "So you didn't find him after all!"

"Sho' didn't, ma'am," was the reply. "An' Ah sho' nuff cain't understan' it. Ah done looked ev'ywhere in de whole house!"

All eyes flew to *Aunt Lydia,* who came in on time with her next important line: "I know *one* place you didn't look!"

Mamma gasped, and the *Yankee Army's* eyes rolled in anticipation.

The Sugar Bowl Game

"In here," said *Aunt Lydia*—and playfully removed the top to the sugar bowl!

That was the way the story had really happened. The children always clapped their hands at the end of the game, partly in approval of themselves but largely because they always felt a sense of pride over Mamma's bravery and Aunt Lydia's touch of humor in the midst of such a dangerous situation.

After they had released *Papa* from his hiding place, Petite remarked: "You know, I don't think we do it just right, hiding Papa's cup behind the drapes. Suppose the Yankees had found it. It would have ruined everything. I wonder what Mamma really did do with it? I guess we'll have to ask her."

9. On the Levee

"Just think," said Lena, "a little while ago, all that water was flowing past Natchez—and in a little while more, it will be going by New Orleans and into the Gulf."

"I've never been to Natchez," said Petite, "but Papa has promised to take me someday. It must be a very interesting place. So far, I've only been *down* the river on a boat."

Lucy didn't say anything. She sat quietly gazing at the wide river below them.

The three girls were sitting on top of the levee above Belle Vale's boat landing. It was Christmas Eve, and Mamma had given them permission to walk as far as the levee to show the river to their guest.

All the Christmas preparations at the house were finished. The children had decorated the mantels with fresh green boughs of magnolia leaves, pine branches and sprays of youpon berries which Jimmie had brought home to them. Over the doorway between the parlor and the dining room they had hung a branch of mistletoe, with a giggle or two over whom they would like to catch beneath it.

Tonight they would all sing Christmas carols around the piano, and Papa would read the Christmas Story to them from the family Bible. Then they would hang their stockings on the parlor mantel and leave a plate of bread, milk and fruit for Santa Claus when he came in the night. Petite knew that Mamma would have a stocking ready for Lucy to hang beside theirs, for guests at Belle

On the Levee

Vale were always made to feel as much as possible a part of the family that lived there.

She stole a glance at the young girl sitting between her and Lena. She was sorry now that she had ever felt jealous over her coming. Lucy was a quiet, likeable girl and although she had been there only a few days, she had already won the affection of every member of the family. Especially had their hearts gone out to her when they learned of the recent loss that had brought her to New Orleans from her former home in St. Louis. An only child, she had lost both parents within the past year. Petite thought of her own large family and the comfort of having so many with whom she could always share her joys and little sorrows. She couldn't even imagine what it would feel like to be so alone in the world. It made her wish that it were somehow possible for her to move over closer in the family circle to allow Lucy a place beside her.

Lena had taken it for granted from the moment of their arrival that Petite would join them in all that they did. All except at night, of course, when she and Lucy slept together in the Guest Room while Petite lay alone in her bed downstairs, wondering what they were talking about up there after the lamps were out—memories of things that had happened at school, their teachers, their friends, and outings they had taken together. Sometimes she couldn't keep a little feeling of envy from creeping into her mind; but she would shake it off immediately, remembering how much she had wanted to come back to Belle Vale.

Lucy was interested in everything about the plantation and kept them all busy answering her questions. In

Sugar Petite

St. Louis she had lived in town, where her father was in the mercantile business; and since her aunt in New Orleans also lived within the city, the country life of which she found herself a part at Belle Vale was new and very fascinating to her.

The girls had enjoyed the past few days, showing her over the plantation. One morning Brother Jimmie had let them ride with him when he went to the fields. Lena had ridden "Molly," one of their favorite saddle horses, while Petite had mounted "Stockings," a dun colored little mare with white stocking-markings on all four of her dainty legs. Lucy, who was less used to riding, was assigned "Old Jim," the younger children's horse who, though too old and slow to be considered much of a mount, was so patient and dependable he often carried as many as three or four children at once. Lucy said that he was just the right speed for her and that his lack of spirit suited her fine.

Petite was pleased and, at the same time, bothered by the way Jimmie was acting these days. He was treating all three of them like real young ladies, and he didn't even tease as much as he usually did. She could tell that Lucy was very much impressed with him, although she was quiet and shy whenever he was near. For a moment, when she first noticed this, Petite's heart had stood still as she frantically counted off on her fingers the difference in their ages—fifteen and twenty-one. Only six years! Papa was nine years older than Mamma, and she had married him when she was exactly Lucy's age! Then she had calmed herself by remembering that that was many years ago. Girls didn't marry that young now-

On the Levee

a-days. However, it did give her a funny feeling when she thought about it.

Jimmie had very carefully explained to them everything about the planting of the fields, which were now all cut over since the harvesting of the crop was finished. He even got off his horse to show them how the cane joints would be planted in the spring and how, after the crop was cut the following fall, it would be allowed to come up by itself for the next two years to be harvested as "stubble cane." Then that field would be plowed up and planted in corn and cowpeas to "rest" it for a year, at the same time furnishing feed for the live stock. He said that by using this method, which was called "rotation," some of the fields were always being rested while others produced cane. Petite learned a lot herself that morning . . .

In the afternoon Papa had let them take the buggy and "Stockings," with Lena holding the reins, and drive to the sugar mill. The road passed by a line of fig trees, back of which were located the Negro cabins—ten small frame houses strung out in a row, known not too many years before as the "slave quarters." Some of the women and children could be seen from the road, and they had waved as the buggy passed by, a greeting affectionately returned by Lena and Petite, who had known most of them all their lives. Papa was proud of the fact that almost all the colored folk had stayed on with the plantation after they were freed from slavery by the War. Petite knew this was a sign that they had been happy, even in the old days, and still had a real sense of belonging there in spite of their new station in life.

At the sugar mill Papa had shown them through, him-

Sugar Petite

self, explaining each step in the process, from the time the cut cane was unloaded from the cane wagons until it was run through the "purgery" and emerged as finished sugar. By the end of December most of the cane had already been ground, but fortunately there was enough left to show Lucy just how it was done. Together they watched the green cane put on the carriers which conducted it through the rollers, the juice falling into tanks below, from which it was then let into kettles over the fires. After being boiled in the first of these kettles, of which there were several, the juice was tested and, when it reached a certain point, was run into the next kettle for further boiling. Only when it showed that it was ready to "sugar," was it run into the wooden containers over the purgery. Papa explained that the drippings which fell into the purgery were used as crude molasses and that the thick grainy syrup in the last kettle was called "la cuite" and was delicious on batter cakes, biscuits, and other hot breads. After promising to give Lucy some of this delicacy to take back to her aunt, since it was not always easy to find it in the city stores, he showed them the huge hogsheads in which the finished brown sugar was stored until time to haul it to the boat landing for shipment to the refinery in New Orleans.

Closer to the house there were also many things to show a newcomer to Belle Vale. There was the Indian mound in the side yard, where the children loved to play, with seldom a thought of the redmen who once used it as a burial place. There were the points of interest in the back yard—the stable and horses, the barn and pond for the cows, the pig pen and the chicken yard. They had spent some time in the orchard and vegetable

On the Levee

garden, where Pinkie had greeted them with such unusual cordiality that it brought forth an unanswered question of surprise from Lena. Petite, also noticing the change in the old man, had smiled happily, feeling sure that she knew the reason. She would never tell, however. This was a secret that belonged to her and Pinkie alone, and even Lena could never share it with them.

Not far from the house, the girls had shown Lucy Papa's "cyclone tunnel," which was regarded by everyone else as a sort of family joke, so many years had it stood there without ever being used. Originally it had been an old smoke stack from the sugar mill—an enormous iron cylinder about twenty-two feet long—and now, resting lengthwise on wooden runners, it would, Papa insisted, give the family safe shelter should a cyclone or tornado visit Belle Vale. Sometimes Petite almost wished that a cyclone would come, just for Papa's sake, to prove that his beloved tunnel was of some use after all. Year after year he saw that it was kept clean and in readiness, but so far it had never been used, except as a place for the children to play.

"I think it's wonderful to live right on the river," said Lucy, finally breaking the silence. "Of course, New Orleans and St. Louis are both on the river, too, but living in a city, you don't realize it the way you do here. Being this close to it makes it seem a real part of your life."

"It *is* a big part of our life here at Belle Vale," replied Lena. "In fact, all the plantations along the river depend on it for ever so many things besides just the good land it gives them. They all have their boat landings like ours, each with a road going over the levee and down

Sugar Petite

the other side. Of course, that's the way they all send their sugar and other produce to New Orleans to be sold. Some of the plantations sell other crops as well as sugar, and some raise live stock for sale; but, except for potatoes and pecans, we don't. The other things we grow are just for the family to use."

"And the things that Belle Vale can't provide for us Papa gets from New Orleans," added Petite. "Ice twice a week, and coal-oil for the lamps, and salt and rice and flour—things like that. They're all unloaded right down there at the boat landing and hauled to the house in the old wagon."

"Don't you ever shop in Baton Rouge?" asked Lucy. "It's so much closer."

"Well, yes, sometimes," admitted Lena. "Of course, it's right down there a little way, across the river. The mail boat from Bayou Sara to Baton Rouge goes by the landing every morning at nine o'clock, except on Sundays, and you can flag it down if you want to and then come back on it at two o'clock in the afternoon. And when it isn't too muddy for horseback, you can ride from here to the ferry and go across that way, too. But we don't go very often. Baton Rouge isn't much of a town—just a few thousand people even if it is the state capital—and the shopping isn't very good. Mamma and Papa usually wait to buy things in New Orleans."

"It's fun to visit friends across the river, though," put in Petite. "We do that sometimes, and sometimes Jimmie and Carrie go to the 'hops' at the University. Of course they spend the night with friends when they go. It's too far to come back the same night . . . Look, there's a flatboat coming down the river!"

On the Levee

The three girls stood up, the better to see the strange looking craft that had just come into view. It was a large, raftlike affair with a square cabin built in the center. Two men stood on the deck holding long poles in their hands.

"Farther up the river," said Lena, "they have to use the poles to help it along, but down here the water is so wide and deep they really don't need them as long as they don't get too near the banks. Papa says there used to be lots of flatboats on the river; but there aren't so many now, what with steamboats and the railroads that are being built everywhere. It's too hard to get them back up the river. Most folks sell them for lumber once they get to New Orleans."

"They make me think of *Huckleberry Finn*," commented Petite. "Have you read it, Lucy? Papa brought it to us from New Orleans. He says Mark Twain's books are the best that have been written since the War."

"I read *Tom Sawyer*," said Lucy, "but I haven't read the new one."

"Papa has another of his books that he wrote just a few years ago. It's called *Life on the Mississippi*, and it's all about the river—all the way up past St. Louis . . ."

She stopped short, fearing for a moment that maybe she shouldn't have mentioned their guest's former home, but her remark went unnoticed.

"I like all kinds of boats," Lucy said, "steamboats and flatboats and sailboats, but most of all I like the showboats. Does the showboat ever stop near here?"

"It stops *right* here!" Lena and Petite answered in duet, which made them all laugh. Lena went on to explain: "Papa lets them use our landing as a stopping place, so

Sugar Petite

the captain always gives free tickets to everyone in the family. Oh, it's wonderful when the showboat comes! People come from all the nearby plantations, and the road along the levee here is full of their carriages. We walk from the house; and when you get to the river, with the showboat all lighted up and the music playing—well, I just don't think anything in the world could be more exciting. Of course, we always see lots of our friends and visit with them before and after the show and during the intermission."

"And sometimes some of our friends spend the night with us if they've come very far," Petite added. "It's so much fun when we get home, talking about the plays and vaudeville acts and who was there, and all."

The wind from the river had risen sharply and was tugging at the girls' skirts and the scarves tied about their heads.

"It's getting cold," said Lena, turning her back to the river and pulling her jacket more closely around her, "and I guess it's getting late, too. We'd better start on back before Mamma worries about us."

Down the levee and across the dirt highway, the girls passed through the wide gate to Belle Vale. The fence bounding the front of the property was entirely overgrown with Cherokee rose vines which formed a thick and impenetrable hedge. A few months from now, it would be covered with thousands of white blossoms shining like stars in the dark green foliage. Inside the gate, the driveway formed a huge circle in front of the house. The area thus enclosed was planted with large pecan trees now bare of leaves, clothed only with the long strands of Spanish moss hanging gracefully from their branches.

On the Levee

As the home came into view, Petite paused for a moment to stand and look at the picture it made in the fading afternoon sunlight. It wasn't an elaborate house —a white, frame building with a wide wooden-railed gallery in front and a shingled roof which, broken by one large curved dormer window, slanted down to a point beyond the gallery where it was supported by six white pillars.

Seeing it now, with its familiar faded green shutters, its precious, magic-colored door panes, the smoke from its six fireplaces forming a cloud above it, and the flicker of lamplight and hearthfire shining from its windows, Petite felt a catch in her heart as she often had before.

"*What if the Yankees had burned it!*" she thought. "*What if it had gone like so many of the plantation homes, and I had never known it!*"

Leaving Lena and Lucy to come more slowly, she caught up her skirt and ran the rest of the way to the welcoming shadows under the roof.

10. Christmas Day

"May Kissmus! May Kissmus!"

Petite awoke from a sound sleep to find Nootsie lying on his small stomach atop her back. Apparently the word as he pronounced it had an entirely original meaning for him. With his fat little arms clamped tightly around her neck, he was smothering her with a deluge of very loud and very wet kisses.

"Nootsie!" she exclaimed, shaking him off with some difficulty and sitting up in bed to hold him in her lap. "Whatever do you think you're doing?"

"Kiss-mus!" repeated the little boy, holding up his face to her, his lips rounded into a rosy pucker. Petite laughed and gave him a hearty kiss. "You're a monkey," she said. "But how did you ever get way up here on this high bed all by yourself?"

In answer to her question, she heard a soft laugh as Julia arose from her hiding place at the foot of the bed. "Merry Christmas, Petite," she said gaily. "Ev'ybody's up but you, an' yo' mamma sent me an' Nootsie in to wake you. De chillun's already into dere stockin's."

"Oh, mercy me!" cried Petite, dumping Nootsie out

Christmas Day

of her lap as she scrambled to the floor. "Are Lena and Lucy up, too?"

"Dey's dressin' now," said Julia. "Dey say to tell you dey's gonna wait fo' you in de parlor."

"Please go tell them I'll hurry," said Petite. "I'll just put on something quick now and really dress later. Oh, how *could* I have overslept on Christmas morning?"

She washed her face in such haste that some of the water splashed out of the bowl and onto the washstand. Quickly mopping it up with the towel, she grabbed her old brown wool dress out of the armoire. She had planned to wear her best new one this morning, but that would call for more time than she had now. She would slip back to her room later on when she wasn't in such a hurry.

It took her only a few minutes to dress and join the other children in the parlor. Eva and Bena were seated on the floor, counting over the piles of apples, oranges, nuts and candies with which Santa Claus had filled their stockings. On the mantel an empty plate showed that he had enjoyed the early breakfast so thoughtfully left for him.

"Merry Christmas!" everyone shouted as she entered the room. Lena and Lucy were already there. "I've never seen anyone dress in such a hurry," said Lena. "Julia just now went in to wake you."

"I know it, and I guess I look like it, too." Petite ran a hand over her untidy hair, which she had unsuccessfully tried to smooth down with a few quick jabs of the comb. "I just couldn't take time really to fix up. Where are Mamma and Papa? Out on the back porch?"

"Goodness, yes," said Lena. "The colored folk have

Sugar Petite

been coming to the house since sun-up. I'm surprised they didn't wake you, they made so much noise."

"I didn't hear a thing until Nootsie jumped on my bed," said Petite. "Let's get our stockings and then go back there, too. I want to tell everybody 'Merry Christmas.' "

The contents of the stockings were never a surprise, for each year they were the same—fruit, nuts and a variety of small sweets—but they never failed to bring forth a scene of great excitement. Each piece was removed separately and was exclaimed over as if it were the greatest treasure in the world. Later they were all returned to the long black stockings, to be kept safe as long as healthy young appetites let them last.

The younger children stopped their play and looked on now as the three girls took turns removing the wonderful array of goodies and placed them in separate piles in front of them. They each sampled a piece of candy as they refilled their stockings and then, going through the kitchen to speak to "Aunt Rachel" and "Aunt Harriet," they made their way to the back porch.

Out here an old table served as an office for Papa every Saturday morning when the colored domestic help came for their wages, the field hands being paid off at the sugar mill. This morning the porch bore a more festive air than usual. On the table Carrie had arranged a spray of youpon berries. Beside it were several whiskey bottles and a bowl full of silver coins. As the colored men from the quarters came to the back door with their cries of "Merry Christmas!" and "Christmas Gif'!" Papa poured for each a drink from one of the bottles and placed a coin in his outstretched hand.

Christmas Day

Mamma was out there, too, adding her cordial greeting to his. Petite kissed them both, feeling a sense of pride in them for taking time on this busy, happy morning to spend a while with their colored folk. That was one reason, she knew, why life at Belle Vale had continued to run fairly smoothly since the War. The unselfish kindness of their master and mistress was returned by the plantation help in devotion and hard work.

After breakfast, which was an especially hearty and enjoyable one in honor of the day, everyone pushed back from the table and waited for Papa to give out the Christmas presents. This was the great moment when the "mystery packages" from New Orleans were brought out of hiding. They were all arranged on the parlor table to be distributed by Papa—each to be accompanied by a hearty kiss and hug, except of course, in the case of Brother Jimmie, who received a grownup man-to-man handshake with his.

Petite thought that the presents had never been as wonderful as this year. For Mamma, Papa had chosen a lovely new winter cloak—a fashionable, long "dolman" of black velvet trimmed in soft fur. Carrie received a new dress which she had selected for herself in New Orleans and had then given to Papa to keep until Christmas Day. Jimmie's package revealed a heavy, gold watch chain on which to wear the watch he had received as a graduation gift. Until now he had worn an old one of Papa's, and this he immediately removed and handed back to him as he proudly arranged the new one across the front of his dark vest. For Lena there was a new handbag and, tucked inside, a box of stylish name cards engraved with "Miss" before her full name, a real sign

Sugar Petite

that she was a grown young lady at last. Lucy was remembered, too, with a dark blue leather autograph book in which to keep the names of all the new friends she was making at school.

The next package that Papa took from the table was a very small, square one tied with bright red ribbon. "And this tiny little bit of a present," he said and then paused, looking all around the room while everyone waited in suspense, "is for our Petite. Merry Christmas, Sugar."

Petite held up her face for his kiss as she took the package from his hand. It was smaller than all the rest, but she sensed immediately that it contained something very special. Mamma and Papa had exchanged a *very special* look as he handed it to her. "Oh, thank you, Papa," she said, holding it ever so carefully as she studied it lying there on her smooth, rosy palm. Then she added: "Do you mind if I wait to see what it is until after all the other presents are opened?" She couldn't explain just why she wanted it that way, but somehow she felt that this was going to be a precious and exciting moment and that she wanted all the other excitement out of the way.

For an instant Papa looked disappointed. Then he seemed to understand and laughed. "All right, Sugar, if that's the way you want it. But maybe you'll be disappointed. Maybe it looks better from the outside!"

Petite sat quietly holding the little package, trying to guess what could be inside.

"Next," said Papa. "Merry Christmas to Miss Eva!" He said it in just the tone he would have used if addressing a grown person, and Eva beamed with pride as she came up to the table.

Christmas Day

"*Oh, I hope it isn't a toy!*" Petite thought prayerfully. When she heard Eva's squeal of joy, she knew that everything was all right. "A muff! A real lady's muff!" In a moment the little girl was skipping all around the room, showing off her lovely new possession. It was of fluffy, white fur with a crimson, quilted satin lining. After each member of the family had admired it, she stopped to bury her nose in its soft warmth before dancing on to the next.

The room still seemed full of her happiness as Papa handed to little Bena the package marked with her name. This time it was a very large one, and Bena added her happy cries to Eva's as she lifted out a beautiful new doll—a young lady doll, her stiff cloth body dressed in a long silk dress with stylish bustle, and a velvet cape around her shoulders. In the box there was also a printed challis dress for everyday wear.

Under the table everyone had been noticing with interest a large package rather clumsily but effectively done up in plain brown paper. Whatever it contained was obviously too large to be wrapped in the traditional white tissue paper and red or green ribbon.

"Come on, Nootsie Boy," said Papa. "Your turn now. Let's pull off the paper."

He pulled the package from under the table as Nootsie came scrambling across the floor on all fours and began jerking at the wrapping. With some help from Papa, the little boy quickly uncovered a brightly painted, wooden rocking horse with a big, red ribbon tied around its neck.

"Horsie, horsie!" squealed Nootsie, immediately mounting it and rocking back and forth so fast that it almost tipped over. A little brass bell tied to the ribbon

Sugar Petite

tinkled merrily as he rocked. But all of a sudden he stopped and pulled down the corners of his mouth. "May Kissmus," he whimpered, looking at Papa.

"You forgot to kiss him, Papa," said Petite. "He thinks the word 'Christmas' has something to do with kissing."

"Well, in this family I think it does," laughed Papa. He gave Nootsie his kiss; then pushed the toy horse to start it rocking again. "Now, Petite, the stage is all yours."

"No, not yet, Papa—Mamma hasn't given you your present yet, and then I have something for her."

From the folds of her dress Mamma produced Papa's gift, which she carried over and almost shyly presented to him. When he unwrapped it, he uttered a cry of surprise. It was a beautiful, ruby-studded, gold scarf pin. He took it from its box and fastened it in his broad cravat. Then he stuck out his chest with an air of pride. "But how . . .?"

"My pecan money," Mamma answered simply. Except for those gathered by the children and the especially fine, rich ones saved for family use from "Papa's Tree" in the front yard, all of the pecans belonged to Mamma. It was understood that whatever money was brought in by the big, lumpy sacks shipped down the river each year, she was to keep for herself, to buy any extra luxury for which she might have been yearning. "I've wanted to get you one ever since you lost yours in New Orleans."

Petite was glad Papa didn't tell her that she shouldn't have done it. He just stood for a minute looking at her. Then he touched his fingers to his lips and laid them over the scarf pin. Everyone could see how much he loved it.

Now she was happier than ever that she had her own

Christmas Day

present for Mamma, as she tenderly placed the shawl around her shoulders and stood back to see how it looked. It was even lovelier on her than she had imagined it would be. The glowing shade of rosy red made a pretty contrast with her white skin, at the same time reflecting some of its color into her pale cheeks.

"I just can't believe it," Mamma said, as she stroked it with her long, slender fingers. "To think that you knitted it for me all by yourself!"

Lena and Lucy came near to admire it. Neither of them could knit like that. It made Petite feel very important to know that she could do something better than they.

"And now," she said, after everyone had finished admiring everyone else's gifts, "now, I'm going to open mine." Carefully she untied the red ribbon and removed the thin paper from around the little box. Inside, lying on a lining of white velvet, was the most beautiful ring she had ever seen—a single, flawless pearl mounted in a gold setting. She held her breath in excitement as she slipped it on her finger.

"Oh," she whispered. "A beautiful pearl—a pearl, just like my name!" Her eyes met her father's and held them in a long look of perfect love and understanding. Then she looked at Eva. The little girl, forgetting all about her new muff, was taking in the scene with a radiant expression of happiness on her small, round face.

"*Now,*" thought Petite gratefully, "*now she can really enjoy the ring I gave her, because I have one that's even prettier!*"

The rest of the day passed quickly. Late in the morning, a plate of fruitcake and a large bowl of eggnog were placed on the buffet in the dining room to keep

Sugar Petite

everyone from getting too hungry while waiting for dinner, which today would not be served until the middle of the afternoon. When the time finally came, it was a meal to be remembered always—chicken and oyster gumbo, baked turkey with rice and cornbread dressing, and also a big roast of pork, candied sweet potatoes, boiled onions and butterbeans; all of this accompanied by hot biscuits and crisp, salted pecans roasted in butter until they were just the right shiny brown. There was wine for the grownups, and after dinner coffee following dessert of ambrosia and fruitcake.

Belle and her family arrived in time for dinner and planned to spend the night with them. Brother Johnny had already sent word that they would not be able to come, since little Lizzie had a touch of "grippe" and they were afraid to take her away from home. Christmas dinner didn't seem right without Johnny there but, as Mamma said, with a family as large as theirs, especially now that there were grandchildren to be considered, too, they couldn't expect to keep on having everyone together for every holiday meal.

As soon as it was dark enough, they all went out on the gallery to watch the Christmas fireworks that Papa always set off in the front yard. Jimmie and Belle's husband helped him, and there was much consulting and running from one large box to another before the first rocket shot high into the air to explode in a burst of stars. The colored folk had gathered in the side yard to watch the show, and their exclamations of "O-o-oh!" and "A-a-ah!" were added to the cheers from the gallery.

Petite was sitting on the front steps. She was enjoying the fireworks but, even more than that, she was enjoying

Christmas Day

thinking back over the wonderful day. Once more she went over in her mind the presents received by the different members of the family. Papa must have been right when he said that this had been an exceptionally good cane year. Had the crop been poor—and she could remember many years when it was—the day would have been just as happy and his Christmas kisses just as warm, but the gifts themselves would have been simpler. She ran a finger over the smooth, round pearl in her ring. She would keep it and love it always, but no one else would ever know the real meaning it held for her and Papa.

One day not very long ago, she had asked him about her name. All the other names in the family seemed so much prettier than hers. Mamma's name was Angelina, although those closest to her called her "Angie" for short. Angelina Adelia—it sounded just like music, like chimes ringing. Lena was really Angelina, too, and there were Carrie Louise and Mary Belle. Bena's real name was Lavenia and even Eva May had sort of a rhythm to it.

"Why," she had asked Papa, "why, when it came time to give me a name, did you and Mamma choose such a short and plain sounding one as 'Pearl'?"

"I'm sorry if you don't like it, Sugar," he had answered seriously, "but maybe you will when I tell you how I feel about it. To me a pearl has always been the most beautiful gem in the world. Oh, there are others more dazzling—diamonds and emeralds and sapphires—but a pearl somehow stands for everything that is fine and lovely and perfect. It's simple and dignified, and it shines with a soft sort of beauty that's different from all the rest. That's why I can't think of a lovelier name for the lovely lady I know you're someday going to be."

Sugar Petite

Tonight as she looked at the gaudy fireworks lighting up the front yard—leaping into the air to fade again so quickly into nothingness—and then felt the solid perfection of the Christmas pearl on her finger, she understood for the first time just what Papa had meant. And suddenly she knew that when the time came for her to stop being called "Petite," she was going to love the name that had been given her.

11. "Dolly Madison's" Funeral

Almost before Petite realized that it was happening, signs of springtime came to Belle Vale. It seemed to her that one day it was cold and dark and wet, and the very next morning the sun came out and with it came the spring. Underneath the dripping moss-hung trees, camellias and azaleas were in bloom; violets were purple bright; and spring bulbs were poking their brave little heads through the damp, dark earth. A newly arrived flock of robins hopped about under the pecan trees in front of the house, while overhead the cardinals that had stayed around all winter called forth with a new note of gay excitement in their song.

Most of the trees began showing signs of awakening, with buds swelling along their branches and some of them putting forth tiny leaves of palest green. In a few more weeks the redbud and dogwood trees would be covered with pink and white blossoms. Only the pecan trees refused to show the slightest sign that there was any change in the time of year. Petite knew that this was because they were smarter than the other trees. They alone seemed to realize that winter wasn't really over and that, as suddenly as it had left, it might return for one last visit, freezing and killing the tender leaves and flowers of the more precocious plants. Only when the pecan trees put out their leaves could everyone be sure that springtime had come to stay.

She found a sleepy-eyed turtle just emerging from its long winter dreams. A careful study of its strangely hinged undershell showed to her delight that it was a

Sugar Petite

box turtle and would therefore make a good pet—much more fun than the common green turtles of which the children found many each year, or the short tempered snappers which experience had taught them to leave strictly alone. She gave the new turtle to Bena, who loved anything alive and was old enough now to enjoy taking care of a pet of her own. Eva wanted to name it "Geronimo," after the bad Indian they had heard Papa and Jimmie discuss so often lately. Petite agreed that "Geronimo" was a beautiful name, but she thought it sounded too long and complicated for a poor little half-grown turtle. After much discussion, they finally compromised by calling it "Gerry," which shortened form of the Indian's name had a happier and more friendly sound.

Usually Petite dreaded the dark days that often followed Christmas—days when sometimes even the big front gallery was too damp and cold for comfortable play. This year, however, the time had passed quickly and happily. After school hours, while the younger children romped and played in their room, on the steps or in the big hall upstairs, she amused herself with a number of pastimes of her own choosing.

She discovered how much she liked to read and buried herself for hours in the fat volumes of Sir Walter Scott recently brought from New Orleans. *Ivanhoe* and *Kenilworth,* with their adventure stories of fair ladies and gallant knights, filled her daytime thoughts and her dreams at night with pictures of a life more exciting than she had ever imagined.

Carrie offered to help her learn to sew. Together they cut out and started work on a dress for her to wear the following summer. It was made of white lawn, soft and

"Dolly Madison's" Funeral

cool, and was going to have rows of tucking down the lace-trimmed front, with the skirt gathered very full in the back to give the popular bustle effect. Carrie was doing most of the dainty hand work, but Petite soon learned to baste an even line and to run up the seams on the wonderful Singer sewing machine that had been Mamma's Christmas gift from Papa several years before. Of course she made mistakes, most of them when her feet got to pushing too hard on the foot treadle that must be worked back and forth to make the machine run. Then she couldn't stop in time, and in her excitement she would lose control of the stitching. But Carrie was very patient, and she knew that gradually she was improving at her work.

Some days, when she grew tired of reading and sewing, she would wander to the kitchen where "Aunt Rachel" was always ready to explain to her the different steps in the preparation of her favorite dishes. She learned just how much flour and how much grease to stir together over the fire until it became the thick, dark "roux" that is the first step in the gumbos, stews and gravies of all good Louisiana cooks. She learned how much water to put on the rice so it would absorb every drop as it steamed and would emerge white and fluffy, with each grain firm and at the same time soft. ("Gummy rice am a sin an' a disgrace," "Aunt Rachel" said. "Ef you cain' cook rice lak it's meant to be cooked, you jes' *cain'* cook, dat's all!") She learned how often to spoon the boiling water over the finely ground coffee in the small French drip coffee pot on the back of the stove, and how to use the long handled wire whisk to beat up egg whites on a large platter until they stood in peaks like snow white mountains in some fairyland.

Sugar Petite

Reading and sewing and cooking—Petite had never cared much for any of them before, but this year they were fun and helped the winter days fly by as if by magic.

One late February afternoon, when the warmth of the early springtime still seemed a thing of wonder, she lay in the old hammock on the front gallery, enjoying the mildly fragrant fresh air from Belle Vale's garden while her mind roamed happily thousands of miles away and hundreds of years ago. She was rereading *Ivanhoe,* for the moment her favorite book. She had just reached the thrilling climax of the tournament scene. The wounded but victorious Disinherited Knight had been revealed as Ivanhoe and had fallen fainting at the feet of the beautiful Lady Rowena, when Petite heard the sound of feet on the wooden steps. Resolutely she kept on reading and didn't look up until she heard Bena's troubled voice, accompanied by an unmistakable sniffle.

"Petite," (sniff)—"I need you!"

"What's the matter?" She sat up and swung her feet over the side of the hammock.

In front of her stood Bena, with drooping mouth and a most mournful expression in her tear-filled brown eyes. Carefully held in her arms was her oldest and most battered looking doll. It was minus one arm, the sawdust stuffing showed through its worn cloth body, and its china head was a network of lines where it had been repeatedly broken and glued together.

"We're gonna bury Dolly Madison—an' I don't want *anybody* to say the prayers 'cept you."

"What?" asked Petite, blinking her eyes in bewilderment. It was hard to adjust herself to the sudden jump from the Middle Ages to a funeral for Dolly Madison.

"Eva says we've gotta bury her 'cause . . . 'cause she's

"Dolly Madison's" Funeral

too beat up to be alive . . . an' I don't want to, unless— Oh, Petite, *please* come!"

Seeing how important it was to her, Petite knew that she couldn't refuse. "Why, of course I'll come," she said quickly, leaving her book in the hammock as she took her place beside her little sister. "Where's Eva?"

"She's already there." (Another sniff) "She's even got the grave dug already." She slipped one hand in Petite's, holding it very tightly for comfort, as together they walked around the house to the back yard.

The "old kitchen," as it was still called, was a frame building set well up off the ground on brick supports, the space underneath being ample to provide a wonderful playroom for the children. For years this had been the chosen spot for the little girls' dolls and doll houses. The houses were all home made, fashioned out of old orange crates placed end to end to form rooms and stacked on top of one another for two story buildings. The furniture was made out of cardboard cut and folded into the desired pieces, with scraps of cloth used for window curtains, rugs, tablecloths and bedspreads.

At one end of the play area the children had made a doll church of which they were very proud. Originally the large, round cake box in which Sister Belle's wedding cake was delivered from New Orleans, it was surrounded by wooden slats. Inside they had furnished it with cardboard pews arranged on either side of a center aisle. There was an altar made of a small, white box on which a tiny wooden cross stood upright in an empty spool. Just outside the church was the doll "grave yard" where the old dolls, either broken or worn out with age and too much fondling, were finally laid to rest in care-

Sugar Petite

fully dug graves covered with mounds of earth and whitewash.

Here Dolly Madison was to find her well-earned resting place. She was, that is, if Eva had her way about it; for Eva had left nothing undone in getting ready to start the funeral in fine style. The church pews were already filled with a strange array of china-headed dolls, both men and women, dressed in an assortment of handmade clothes barely showing their dainty china hands and painted shoes. There were no "store bought" babies small enough to belong to these families, so the girls had made their own out of bits of cloth which they had stuffed and dressed. Some of these peculiar looking offspring were placed beside their parents now, and all of them—both old and young—were lying down, since it was impossible to seat them upright in the rather flimsy cardboard pews. Petite thought it looked like a very comfortable way to go to church.

Outside in the cemetery, a new grave was dug—this one larger than the rest, for Dolly Madison was one of the larger dolls. Beside it lay a can of dirt mixed with whitewash which Eva must have begged from one of the colored help. Yes, thought Petite, Eva had really thought of everything to make this funeral a fine one. And yet, as she looked at Bena still clutching poor Dolly, she wasn't at all sure they were doing the right thing.

"Bena," she asked, "do you really *want* to bury her?"

Bena hesitated. "I don't know," she said slowly, "I sorta do an' I sorta don't. I still love her—but Eva says. . ."

"She really doesn't need her any more," put in Eva quickly. " 'Specially now that she has her new Christmas doll, she's got too many children to take care of."

"Dolly Madison's" Funeral

"But Mamma an' Papa have lots of children," reasoned Bena, "an' they keep 'em all. Every time they get a new one, they don't *not* need one they already have!"

Eva could find no answer to this very logical argument, so she hurried on to another: "Well, anyway, you can take one look at her and tell she's ready to be buried. She just couldn't be that busted up and still be alive. And you've gotta bury people pretty quick when they die. It's just not decent if you don't. . . ."

"Oh hush, Eva," interrupted Petite crossly, seeing that Bena was getting more and more upset. "Let me talk to her a minute. Listen, honey, you don't have to bury her if you don't want to. Dolls don't really die the way people do, because they're never really alive. You just pretend what they are. If you want to pretend that Dolly Madison has died, then we'll bury her and put nice flowers on her grave, and you won't have to worry anymore about her being all cracked up. But if you want to pretend she's still alive—well, you'll almost have to play like she's sick all the time 'cause, like Eva says, she does look pretty bad."

Bena thought very hard. Finally she said, "If people are awful sick an' can't ever get well again, sometimes it's better for them to die an' go to Heaven where they'll be happy. Mamma said so once."

Petite and Eva both nodded hopefully.

"Let's bury her," said the little girl, suddenly fired with an unexpected burst of enthusiasm. "Let's bury her right now!"

The funeral service went quickly after that. Together they said the Lord's Prayer and sang one verse of "Jesus, Lover of My Soul," which was one of the few hymns they all knew by heart. When Bena asked Petite to say a

Sugar Petite

special prayer, she decided to make it a short one to avoid any possibility of another change of mind. With bowed head and folded hands, she reverently repeated her favorite bedtime prayer:

> "Gentle Jesus, meek and mild,
> Look upon a little child.
> Pity my simplicity,
> Teach me, Lord, to come to Thee.
> Fain would I to Thee be brought.
> Lamb of God, forbid it not;
> In the Kingdom of Thy grace
> Give a little child a place. Amen."

"Is that all?" asked Bena, sounding disappointed.

"I think that's enough," Petite answered. "Papa says long funerals are too hard on everyone. Now, Eva, you and Bena can put her in the grave."

She started crawling over toward the front of the building. She really wanted to stay to watch the rest of the game, but there was something that she felt needed investigation. Just as she said "Amen," she had heard, close outside, a muffled but very distinct sneeze. Someone was listening to them as they played!

She stuck her head from under the house and, with a start, came face to face with Pinkie who was crouching on the ground close by. So surprised were they both that for a moment neither spoke. Then she asked in a disapproving voice, "Why, Pinkie, what on earth are you doing here?" She knew that Papa would be furious if he should catch the old man eavesdropping on their play.

Pinkie gathered himself up and started looking around on the ground. "Ah . . . Ah's jes' sarchin' fo' sumpin'," he muttered, looking so confused and embarrassed that

"Dolly Madison's" Funeral

she couldn't help feeling sorry for him. "Ah thought Ah'd drapped sumpin' right here an' . . . an' Ah was sarchin' fo' it."

Petite pretended to look too, just to make him feel better, although she knew in her heart that he wasn't telling the truth. "Well, it's not here," she announced at last, "Whatever it was, it's not anywhere here."

"What's the matter?" asked Bena and Eva, leaving poor half-buried Dolly as they, too, came over to find out what was going on.

"Oh nothing," Petite hastily assured them. "It was just Pinkie, looking for something he's lost."

However, she watched with a worried expression on her face as her strange old friend retreated with a shuffling gait toward the safety of his vegetable garden.

The house at Belle Vale

Papa

Charlie

Petite grows up

12. A Prayer for Pinkie

The pecan trees were right. As suddenly as it had left, wintertime came out of its brief hiding to enfold the unwilling countryside in a final freezing embrace. Azalea and camellia blossoms clung limply to the bushes, their beautiful colors turned a wilted brown. Cold winds tore at the tender, pale green lace on the over-confident trees. The fig trees lost their crop of tiny, new formed fruit and would have to start all over a second time. In the front yard the robins fluffed themselves into cold balls of misery, dreaming of the warmer climate they had so foolishly left behind.

In the middle of a stormy night, Petite awoke to hear the wind whistling around the corner of the house and shaking the shutters outside her bedroom windows. Then she realized that the wind alone had not awakened her. In the next room Mamma and Papa were talking, and for one of the few times she could remember, Mamma's voice was raised in argument. She looked across at Carrie's bed, dimly outlined by the lamplight from the next room. It was empty.

"But, my dear," Mamma was saying, "in the middle of the night! And with such a storm going on out there—"

Papa's voice sounded firm as he answered. "I think you know, Angie, that I'd be the last one in the world to take her if I didn't feel sure it was perfectly safe. The wind is blowing hard, but it's not raining. She'll be all wrapped up, warm and protected, in the buggy. Steve has already gone to get it."

A Prayer for Pinkie

"But to take her to one of the cabins to see a sick old man!"

Petite propped herself up on one elbow and listened with interest. Just what were they talking about?

" 'Aunt Rachel' keeps her cabin as neat as a pin," said Papa, "and I've already told you I'm sure there's nothing wrong that anyone could possibly catch. He hasn't had any fever or signs of anything contagious. Of course, I've made sure of that."

"But she's still just a little girl!"

Papa lowered his voice in reply, and Petite had to strain her ears to catch what he was saying. "That isn't the point. The point is that, for some reason, old Pinkie thinks he needs her, and I know she'd want to go. Whether she realizes it or not, Angie, Petite is trying hard within herself to take the step over into the grown-up world. An experience like this is sometimes good for a child, even if it is distressing at the time."

At the mention of Pinkie's name, Petite had waited no longer. By the time Papa finished what he was saying, she had reached the bedroom door and stepped inside. They all looked at her as she entered the room. Mamma was still in bed, sitting up with a shawl around her shoulders as she watched Papa dress. Carrie, in wrapper and slippers, was standing quietly beside her. In the baby bed, Nootsie was still sleeping soundly, unconscious of anything going on around him.

"What's the matter?" asked Petite. In her heart she already knew, but she didn't want anyone to suspect that she had been listening.

"It's Pinkie," said Papa, putting on his coat. "He's sick, and 'Aunt Rachel' and Steve can't do anything with him. He's asked for you, Sugar, and they think if he

Sugar Petite

could just see you, maybe he'd quiet down. I was going to wake you. I thought you'd want to go to him."

Petite felt her heart jump into her throat, and she swallowed hard before answering. "Of course I want to go. I don't know what good I can do; but if he wants me, of course I'll go to him. Is . . . is he very sick, Papa?"

"Well, yes and no, I think," said Papa. "I'll tell you about it on the way."

Carrie helped her dress in her warmest clothes and winter coat, and insisted on tying a woolen scarf about her head. Before she left, she went in to give Mamma a reassuring kiss.

"Don't worry about me, Mamma. I'll be all right. And . . . and I *do* have to go to Pinkie. He's my friend, and he thinks he needs me. Don't let her worry, Carrie," she begged as she left the room.

The ride with Papa that night was the most exciting thing that had ever happened to her. Jimmie helped them into the buggy which he and Steve had made ready for them while they dressed. As they headed down the drive and through the gate to the highway, the wind whipped the sides of the buggy and blew "Molly's" mane and tail into straight lines. But inside, snuggled close against Papa, with a warm blanket tucked around her knees, she felt cosy and safe. They were travelling at a slow, jogging pace, timed to the steps of Steve who was walking ahead of them with a lantern to light the way.

"What time is it?" she asked, peering outside at the unnatural looking landscape.

"About two o'clock, I think," answered Papa. "It was one-thirty when Steve came to the back door."

Petite's heart gave another excited jump. Never in

A Prayer for Pinkie

her whole life had she been out of doors at two o'clock in the morning. And here she was now, riding through the black night to . . . to just what she wasn't sure. It all seemed like part of a very exciting dream.

The night, she decided, wasn't as bad as it had seemed when they were indoors. Overhead the tree branches were tossing in the wind, but high in the sky there was a pale moon that showed its face from time to time as the rushing clouds left it for a moment free.

Then she remembered Pinkie. "Tell me about him, Papa," she said. "What's the matter with Pinkie? You . . . you don't think he's going to die, do you?" For the first time she realized, with a sickening sensation of fear, how urgent might be the call they were answering.

"No, I don't think so," he reassured her. "And I really don't think he's so very sick; that is, I don't think his *body* is very sick." He pulled on the reins, heading "Molly" through the gate to the sugar mill road. "He had a sick spell a few days ago, pretty bad while it lasted —some kind of acute indigestion, I'd say—but he got over that all right. I saw him several times and gave him some medicine. I didn't ever think he was sick enough to send for a doctor. And now—well, now it seems he's just decided he's going to die."

He turned to look at his little daughter. "You probably don't know it, Sugar, but Pinkie is full of all kinds of superstitions and crazy notions."

"Yes, I do know," said Petite emphatically.

Papa gave her a hard, funny look but went on without comment. "Well, you see, what people *think* can have a tremendous effect on how they *feel*. That's where the only real power of Black Magic lies. If a person really believes hard enough in some of those ridiculous charms and cures, sometimes they may actually make him feel better. But, on the other hand, if he really believes hard enough that something bad is going to happen to him . . ."

"I think I understand," interrupted Petite. "Pinkie's just got himself scared to death. Is that it?"

"I think that's it," said Papa, "but I can't be sure. I'm not certain what we'll find when we get there, honey, but I think we ought to go see. Steve seems so sure that just seeing you might help . . . I'll stay right with you. And if things get too bad, we can always leave."

They turned off the road onto the flat, grassy ground beside it. Just beyond was the row of cabins. In the nearest of them a light was burning brightly.

"Here we are, Sugar," said Papa, getting out first and helping her from the buggy. "We'll have to walk the rest of the way." Following Steve and the lantern, they cautiously made their way to the cabin door.

"How is he?" asked Papa as "Aunt Rachel" let them in. Petite looked around the room with interest. It was the first time she had ever been in one of the Negro cabins. She had been in the Tripletts' house in the back yard, but the ten cabins back of the fig trees were never visited by the white children.

The cabin, she observed, was simple but well-constructed, with unpainted wooden walls, a bare cypress plank floor, and a brick fireplace that served both for heat and cooking. An assortment of cooking utensils rested beside the hearth, and from a big, black pot hung close to the fire came the familiar odor of some of "Aunt Rachel's" savory soup. A low wooden bed in one corner, a crude armoire against a wall, a cupboard, table, and several chairs made up the furnishings of the room. All

A Prayer for Pinkie

were handmade, probably by Steve himself, who was often called upon to do simple carpentry work around the big house.

An opening off one end of the room led to a smaller one beyond. Pinkie must be in there, thought Petite; and she shuddered in spite of herself as she heard a low, moaning sound coming through the door.

"He ain't doin' no good at all," said "Aunt Rachel," answering Papa's question in a low voice. "He ain't got no fever, but he say he's still got de stummick cramps. He won't eat nothin' at all. Ah's tried an' tried to get him jes' to try a little of mah broth, but he jes' lie dere moanin' an' groanin'. Ah's done all Ah can think of to help him . . ."

"Did you get all that stuff from around his neck?" asked Papa, casting an anxious glance in Petite's direction.

"No suh, we didn't. We tried, but he wouldn't give it to us. Mattah of fact, he's got even mo' dan when you was heah. But now he done give up any of dat doin' him no good." She turned to Petite. "Ah sho' hates it, honey chile, sendin' Steve fo' you lak dis. But Pinkie ben askin' an' askin' fo' you—all night he ben askin'. He keep sayin' sumpin' 'bout a prayer he want you to say fo' him—keep beggin' ovah an' ovah: 'Please fetch me Petite. Please fetch me Petite to say me her prayer.' We done tried ev'ything else," she added in an apologetic tone. "Does you know what he mean wantin' yo' prayer?"

"Yes, I think I know," Petite said slowly. She knew that it must be the prayer she had said at the doll's funeral, the day she had caught him eavesdropping on their play, *'Gentle Jesus, meek and mild, look upon a*

Sugar Petite

little child'—What a strange prayer for an old man to be requesting! But maybe, after all . . . "Take me to him," she said.

As they entered the small room, her heart was beating very fast. She wasn't at all sure that she was going to know what to do. But then she saw Pinkie and forgot all about herself. He was lying on a small cot, his head propped against a clean, white pillow. The bed was covered with a dark quilt and there was a small blanket thrown around his shoulders; but, even so, the old man was shaking as if with a chill. From time to time he would take a long, choppy breath and exhale it with a moan. His eyes were closed.

"What's that under the bed?" asked Papa, looking at a tub half-protruding from under the cot. It was filled with water in which were floating large blobs of something white.

"Aunt Rachel" looked shamefaced. "Dat's stale bread in watah," she answered. "He say it's fo' his stummick cramps. Ah knows Ah shouldn't a give it to him—but he beg so pitiful . . ."

Petite put her hand on her father's arm. He looked ready to explode, and it wouldn't help any for him to lose his temper now. Pinkie was already troubled and frightened half to death. "Papa," she said, "please let me talk to him by myself."

As she went to the bedside, suddenly the whole room seemed to change itself into a big stage. The flicker of the candle in the tin sconce on the wall, the old man under the faded patchwork quilt, "Aunt Rachel" and Steve standing in the doorway, even Papa—they all seemed part of an amazing make-believe play in which she was taking a leading role. And because she, too, no

A Prayer for Pinkie

longer seemed entirely real, somehow she stopped feeling frightened and unsure of herself.

"Pinkie," she said gently, "it's Petite. Papa brought me to see you."

The old man opened his eyes. "Lawd bless you, li'l Miss," he said weakly. "Lawd bless you fo' comin'. Ole Pinkie's time done come . . . Ole Pinkie gonna die fo' sho'."

His pinkish, gnarled fingers plucked at the bedclothes.

"How do you know, for sure?" asked Petite. "Did you hear a screech owl near the house, or a rooster crowing at the back door? Or maybe a dog howling with his head to the sky?" She searched her mind for all the signs of death that Pinkie had ever told her. "Or did you maybe dream about pulling a tooth?" She glanced at Papa, who was looking at her with his mouth wide open in amazement.

Pinkie drew a long, broken breath. He was trembling worse than ever. "Ah's heard de voice o' death a-callin'," he moaned. "Ah's tried all de chahms an' dere ain't no help lef' in 'em. Ole Pinkie's time done come . . ." He paused and then whispered, "De prayer, Petite. Ah wants you to say de prayer fo' me; de one you said at de li'l funeral—"

Petite thought again of the prayer, and all at once it no longer seemed a strange one for Pinkie. For quite suddenly she realized that that's what he was—just like a little child, simple and very much afraid. In the *Big Book* in heaven she felt sure that Pinkie, with the excuses for his behavior written opposite his name, was still listed in the children's part.

"I'll say the prayer for you, Pinkie," she said very seriously. "I'll say it for you just as you want. But first there's something we have to do. First we must get rid of

Sugar Petite

all the charms around your neck and under the bed and wherever you have them."

Pinkie cried out in protest and clutched the bedclothes in a gesture of panic.

"You must listen to me, Pinkie," Petite went on calmly. "You must listen to every word I say. I don't think you're really sick at all. I think you just feel this bad because—well, because God is angry with you for believing all the things you do.

"I don't think He's so *very* angry," she added quickly, as the old man looked more frightened than ever, "because I think He knows that you just don't understand about things. But I'm going to tell you right now so you *will* understand and after that—well, after that, it'll just be up to you.

"Pinkie," she took a step nearer the bed, "nobody but God knows when any of us is going to die. It says that in the Bible. You or "Aunt Rachel" or Steve or Papa or me—none of us can know. And if God won't tell us, why do you think He'd tell an owl or a rooster or an old dog? A dog howls 'cause there's a full moon in the sky, and an owl—well, I guess it's just talking to another owl. And if a rooster crows on the back steps, it's just 'cause that's where he happened to be when he felt like crowing. None of it has anything to do with what's going to happen to people."

The trembling grew less as Pinkie listened.

"And about these charms," she continued, "God has told us He wants us to trust in Him. He made us and loves us and wants to take care of us, if we'll just let Him. But all these charms mean that you're putting your trust in something else, and in something so—so *trashy!*" she exploded, unable to think of any other word.

A Prayer for Pinkie

"Hunks of bread floating around in water! You know what I think, Pinkie?" she lowered her voice, wishing that Papa and Steve and "Aunt Rachel" didn't have to be standing there. "You were worried about the devil being in you. Well, the way you *look* has nothing to do with the devil, but the way you're *acting* and *feeling* now has. I think the devil just loves all these charms because they keep you from trusting in God. And God is the only one who can really make you well again."

To her surprise she saw Pinkie reach up and take from around his neck a worn out, blackened looking piece of rope tied with many knots. These, she thought, must be the nine knots he had told her would cure a headache.

"Give it to me," she said sternly, and then changed her mind as she took a closer look. "Come here, Steve, *you* take it!"

Steve took the rope from the trembling hands, and they all stared as Pinkie then removed another string on which two dark objects were fastened.

"What's that?" asked Petite.

"Dem's nutmegs," volunteered "Aunt Rachel." "He say dem's good fo' heart trouble."

"Well, take them, too," Petite instructed Steve, "and then dump out that mess under the bed. Dump it clear out the back door!"

Pinkie watched as Steve carried out her instructions. His air of reluctance was gone. It seemed to Petite that he even looked a bit relieved.

"Is that all?" she asked, as Steve returned with the empty tub.

"One mo'," announced Pinkie in a voice that sounded not only stronger but quite cheerful. He grinned feebly

Sugar Petite

and seemed almost pleased with himself as he reached under the covers and pulled out a small, brown cloth bag.

"Mah root bag," he exclaimed, holding it high. "Bag full o' trashy ole roots—no good!" He dropped it into Steve's waiting hand.

"You see," said Petite, taking advantage of his change of mood. "You feel better already, don't you? That's because you've turned your back on the devil, and God's glad of what you've done."

Her old friend relaxed against the pillow.

"I'll say the prayer for you now," she said simply, and repeated with bowed head:

> *"Gentle Jesus, meek and mild,*
> *Look upon a little child,*
> *Pity my simplicity,*
> *Teach me, Lord, to come to Thee.*
> *Fain would I to Thee be brought,*
> *Lamb of God, forbid it not;*
> *In the Kingdom of Thy Grace*
> *Give a little child a place. Amen."*

Across the room she knew that the others were standing with their heads bowed, too. When she looked up, Pinkie's eyes were closed and he was breathing easily. For a moment she thought that he was asleep, but he spoke as she turned away: "De song, Petite. Could you, please ma'am, sing me jes' a li'l bit?"

She sent an imploring look across the room. "Please help me, Papa," she asked. "He wants 'Jesus, Lover of My Soul'. Please come help me sing it for him." Suddenly she realized that she was very tired. She wasn't sure that she could sing it alone.

A Prayer for Pinkie

He came and stood beside her. She was glad that they had often sung this hymn together, with the whole family gathered around the piano in the parlor; and that, together now, they would both feel sure of the words. He placed a reassuring arm around her as they began:

> "Jesus, Lover of my soul,
> Let me to thy bosom fly,
> While the nearer waters roll,
> While the tempest still is high:
> Hide me, O my Saviour, hide,
> Till the storm of life be past;
> Safe into the haven guide,
> O receive my soul at last."

Papa had a nice voice. Sometimes it boomed a little too loud when he sang, especially in this hymn when he came to the part about the waters rolling and the tempest being high, but tonight he was keeping it soft and just right. He gave her a comforting squeeze as they started the second verse:

> "Other refuge have I none,
> Hangs my helpless soul on thee;
> Leave, ah! leave me not alone,
> Still support and comfort me!
> All my trust on thee is stayed;
> All my help from thee I bring;
> Cover my defenceless head
> With the shadow of thy wing."

That should be enough, thought Petite, longing to be through with this strange night and safe at home again; but Papa went on without stopping. Perhaps he was

Sugar Petite

realizing, as she was, how perfectly right all the words seemed to be. She knew that from now on this would always be Pinkie's hymn; that she would never sing it again wihout thinking of him.

> *"Plenteous grace with thee is found,*
> *Grace to cleanse from every sin;*
> *Let the healing streams abound,*
> *Make and keep me pure within.*
> *Thou of life the fountain art,*
> *Freely let me take of thee:*
> *Spring thou up within my heart,*
> *Rise to all eternity. Amen."*

This time Pinkie's eyes didn't open. He was sleeping the quiet, untroubled sleep of a child.

"Give him some of your broth when he awakes," Papa said to "Aunt Rachel" as they tiptoed to the cabin door. "I think he'll wake up hungry."

The wind had died down and the moon was shining brightly as the buggy carried them home. Steve had stayed behind, his lantern no longer necessary for "Molly" to find the way.

Petite snuggled close against Papa. She was sleepy and tired and very happy. Pinkie had needed her and had called for her and, for the second time, she had given him the comfort he could find nowhere else. She was glad that Papa wasn't asking any questions about all the strange things she had already known. After the first look of surprise on his face, he had seemed to take it quite for granted. And she was very glad that he was saying nothing about being proud of her for the way she had handled the situation. Without his putting it

A Prayer for Pinkie

into words, she could feel it in the straight set of the shoulder against which she rested her sleepy head.

13. The Hurricane

"Eva, please be careful how you cut out the pieces of cloth," begged Petite. "The last one was so little I could hardly sew it around the egg."

"Well, I can't help it, can I," Eva pouted, "if the old hens lay some eggs bigger than others? They ought to lay 'em all the same size."

The two girls were sitting at the table in the dining room. It was the week before Easter, and they were getting ready to color the supply of eggs for the family. In front of Eva was a pile of cloth scraps, carefully saved all year from the family sewing, some of them of solid colors and others of printed material. As she cut each piece to the right size, she handed it across the table to Petite who, armed with needle and thread, carefully and snugly sewed it, with the printed side turned in, around one of the eggs in the large bowl in front of her.

After this step was completed, they would take the gaily dressed eggs to the kitchen where, with "Aunt Rachel's" help, they would hard boil them in a pot of water mixed with wood ashes. And presto! When the pieces of cloth were later removed, each egg would, as if by magic, be dyed or marked with the print of the cloth.

On Easter morning the children would find them mysteriously hidden all over the parlor and dining room and, after the fun of the hunt, each would carefully guard the supply he had found, to be used later for "tucking." Petite wasn't to realize until she was grown that "tucking" Easter eggs was not a universal part of

The Hurricane

the glorious day, and that in many parts of the country the custom was unknown.

In the tucking contest, which usually took place at the breakfast table, each child selected an egg with which to start and, holding it firmly in his hand with one end exposed, gave it a sound tap on the end of an opponent's egg. The procedure was then repeated with the other end, after which the two eggs were examined for damage. Whichever one remained unbroken was the winner, its owner adding the cracked egg to his collection before challenging another player. In this way the eggs rapidly changed hands, and sometimes one with an unusually thick shell could gain possession of almost all the others.

"That looks like a good one," said Eva, reaching across the table with her scissors to point out a large egg with a darkish, coarse-looking shell. "I hope I find that one Easter morning. Last year I won nine eggs and I want to do even better this time."

"I should think you'd want someone else to win this year," Petite commented dryly. "I hope Bena wins the most 'cause she hasn't played as many years as we have."

"Maybe not, but she has more years ahead of her to play," reasoned Eva. "In a little while, we'll be grown up and too old—and then Bena and Nootsie will have all the fun."

"Oh dear," sighed Petite, not wanting to continue the conversation. "I do wish Carrie were here."

Carrie had gone across the river to visit friends in Baton Rouge and was planning to stay until after the church service on Good Friday. Usually she did the sewing part of the Easter eggs, and already Petite's fingers were tired from the unaccustomed work. Then, too, she longed for Carrie for another reason. Something

Sugar Petite

strange was going on that she didn't understand and didn't like at all.

To begin with, it was a terrible day—dark and rainy, with the wind coming in hard, strong gusts. Papa was staying at home. That, in itself, was not strange because usually on days when the weather was too bad for him to go to the fields or sugar mill, he stayed in the house, working at his desk in the hall or reading one of his favorite books in the parlor. Today, however, his behavior was very peculiar. For the past hour he had spent most of the time out on the gallery, watching the sky. Several times Jimmie had gone out there with him, and they had talked together very seriously, although she couldn't hear what they were saying. Once she had gone to the window to look out, and what she had seen had frightened her—great masses of dark, angry looking clouds boiling low in the sky and the trees tossing their branches as if possessed. She had started to tell Eva that she was worried but had changed her mind, not wanting to frighten her, too.

A short time ago, Brother Jimmie had left the house in the midst of the storm, and Papa had gone into the bedroom to talk with Mamma. She could hear "Aunt Rachel's" voice in there, too, and it sounded loud and excited. If only Carrie were here! Petite didn't like the feeling of responsibility that went with being the oldest of the girls left at home.

She pushed her chair back from the table, trying to decide whether or not she should go consult with Papa, when all at once she saw something that made her jump up in alarm. Julia and Indie were carrying a feather mattress through the hall, toward the back porch. At the same moment, the plantation bell began to ring.

The Hurricane

This was all that was needed to complete her fright. Ever since she could remember, she had been used to the sound of the big old bell that rang each morning to send the field hands to their work, at noon to call them home for dinner and again for their return to the fields, and as a final summons in the evening when their daily labors were over. But on a rainy day like this and at this strange hour, it could mean only one thing—Papa was using it as a signal of danger!

She flew across the hall to her parents' room, with Eva following in dismay at her heels.

"Papa! Mamma! What's happening?"

Mamma was putting Nootsie's wraps on him. She seemed calm, but Petite noticed that she was pale and that her eyes held a frightened look. On the day bed sat Bena, all bundled up in a cloak, a look of complete bewilderment on her little face.

Somehow, Papa seemed bigger than usual, perhaps because his voice was big with decision. "You children and your mother are to go to the cyclone tunnel," he announced bluntly. "Julia and Indie are getting it ready now. I'm afraid we're in for a bad blow. You girls go get some kind of wraps to protect you from the rain."

He turned toward the door. Petite knew that he was busily lining up in his mind all the things he must do in this emergency, but she ran to him and caught him by the arm. "You must come with us Papa. Where are you going to be?" Her voice broke as she asked it, and she felt the tears rush to her eyes.

Papa turned and saw the distress written on her face. "I'll be all right, Sugar," he said, taking time to become his more gentle self again. "Julia is going with you to help with the children, but I'll stay here with the domes-

Sugar Petite

tic help and the Triplett family. Jimmie and Steve have gone to send all the rest to the sugar mill, and they'll stay there with them. We're ringing the bell to make them understand that it's important that they go. They'll be safer in the mill than in their cabins," he added, "because the building is made of brick."

" *'He huffed and he puffed but he couldn't blow down the little brick house',"* thought Petite and wished, for the first time in her life, that their house had been made of brick like so many of the more pretentious plantation homes. Then the thought of leaving Papa behind rushed over her like a huge, dark wave.

"Well, I won't go unless you do," she wailed. "If you won't come, I'll stay here, too, and . . . and blow away with you!"

"Don't be ridiculous, Petite." He sounded in a hurry again. "No one is going to blow away. I'm just sending you and your mother to the tunnel because I'll worry less about you there. There are things here that may need my attention. I have to stay, and you can't stay with me. I want you with your mother—" He threw Mamma a concerned glance. "Take care of her for me, Sugar. Don't let the little ones crawl all over her. You and Julia, between you, can manage them. Now, all of you, to the back door! And no one is to be afraid. Everything's going to be all right."

A few minutes later, Mamma, Julia and all the children were settling themselves on the two mattresses that had been placed on the floor of the shelter. They were all wet and out of breath, for they had had to run through the strong wind and driving rain. At the last minute Papa had instructed them to take off their shoes and

The Hurricane

stockings and carry them under their cloaks so, although their feet were wet and muddy, they soon had them dry again. The children begged to be allowed to stay barefooted, and Mamma consented since they were all warm and protected on the big mattresses.

It seemed strange and weird inside the tunnel, with the world outside so dark and dismal, and the rain making a terrific racket beating against the metal top and sides. By now the wind was a steady roar, and the rain was a solid sheet of water. It was a good thing that Papa had chosen a high spot in the yard for the tunnel and had placed it on thick wooden runners. Otherwise, they would have had a stream running from one end to the other. Every once in a while there was a loud crack followed by a crashing sound, as the branch of a tree gave way to the fury of the storm.

There was little head room in the shelter. Mamma, Julia and the two older girls were forced to assume a half-lying position on the mattresses, while Bena and Nootsie could crawl around on their hands and knees. Petite could barely see Mamma in the dim light but she sensed that she was miserable and worried about the rest of the family. Nootsie had crawled over and was trying to climb on her lap.

"Come here, Nootsie," coaxed Petite, remembering what Papa had said. "Come sit by me, and I'll sing you a song."

"Wanna sit Mamma's yap," insisted the little boy, clinging tightly to his mother.

"Come sit on my lap, and I'll give you one of the cookies 'Aunt Rachel' sent with us."

"I'll come," volunteered Bena, who had also been

Sugar Petite

cuddled close to Mamma. She started crawling over to the mattress where Petite was lying.

This was too much for Nootsie. Seeing himself in danger of having his sister get ahead of him with the cookies, he came scrambling over on all fours. "Me tummin'! Me tummin'!" he squealed as he came.

"I'll tell you what let's do," said Petite. "Julia, you go over on the other mattress with Mamma and take care of her while Eva, Bena, Nootsie and I stay on this one. Then we'll sing and tell stories and eat cookies and . . . and play like it's a party." She tried to sound enthusiastic, although she realized that nothing could seem much less like a party than the uncomfortable situation in which they now found themselves. She put her arms around Nootsie and pulled him onto her lap. Bena snuggled against her side, and even Eva seemed to forget for once that she wanted to be grown-up as she, too, crept over to sit close to the little group.

"Aren't you scared, Petite?" she asked, not quite trusting the cheery note that her sister had forced into her voice.

"Of course not," Petite lied bravely. "Didn't you hear Papa say that we mustn't any of us be afraid?"

But just then something hit the tunnel with a terrific crash and Bena began to cry. "Well, *I'm* scared," she sobbed. "I wanta go back in the house!"

"Oh, no we don't!" Petite put an arm around her little sister, hoping that she wouldn't notice how badly it was trembling. "All these years Papa's been keeping this cyclone tunnel just to protect us if ever we needed it and —well now we do and . . . and here we are. It wouldn't be fair to him if we didn't stay."

The Hurricane

She realized that her argument didn't sound very convincing; but it seemed to satisfy Bena, who settled against her arm with a small, resigned sniffle.

"Now, let's all have a cookie, and then we'll sing. Singing's always a good idea when you have troubles."

She opened the box that "Aunt Rachel" had thrust into her hands as they left the house, and handed a cookie to each of the children. "You all right, Mamma?" she asked. "You want a cookie?"

"No thank you, dear, but I . . . I'm all right."

"Cookies is good for troubles, too," commented Bena, munching loudly on hers.

"Now, what shall we sing first?" asked Petite. "How about 'Go Tell Aunt Tabby'?" This seemed to satisfy everyone, so she started them off:

> "*Go tell Aunt Tabby,*
> *Go tell Aunt Tabby,*
> *Go tell Aunt Tabby*
> *De ole grey goose is dead.*
>
> "*De one dat she was savin',*
> *De one dat she was savin',*
> *De one dat she was savin'*
> *To make a feather bed.*
>
> "*Now pore Aunt Tabby,*
> *Now pore Aunt Tabby,*
> *Now pore Aunt Tabby*
> *Won't have her feather bed.*"*

---

*For this and other songs, see "Songs and Games from Belle Vale," beginning page 170.

Sugar Petite

"That doesn't make me feel better," said Eva sadly. "I think it's pitiful about the goose bein' dead and poor Aunt Tabby not havin' her feather bed. It doesn't help my troubles at all!"

"Oh, well," said Petite. "Then let's try 'Down Mobile'."

It took quite a while to sing this one, which had many verses to go with the chorus, some of them composed throughout the years by the colored folk of the plantation. By the time they had finished, Nootsie was sound asleep on her lap. She laid him gently on the mattress and stretched her tired arms.

Next they decided to sing "Ole Aunt Jemimy," but it, too, seemed to sadden Eva, with each line ending "Ole Aunt Jemimy, pore ole soul."

"Why does it call her 'pore ole soul'?" she wanted to know. "What's the matter with her?"

They tried several others, but all seemed to have the same effect. Even "Big-Eye Rabbit," which had always been her favorite, failed to please her. When they came to the part that said:

> "Gotta pain in mah finger,
> Gotta pain in mah toe,
> But mah ole missus call me
> So Ah mus' go,"

Eva protested loudly: "That makes me feel just *awful!* It makes my finger and toe hurt, too!"

Suspecting that she was just acting difficult to cover up the fact that she was frightened, Petite tried to be patient with her, although she wanted to tell her that she was acting even younger than Bena.

The Hurricane

"Well, let's not sing any more," she said. "Maybe we're just not in the mood for it." She didn't feel in the mood for anything except to go in the house and see what was happening to Papa, but Bena was beginning to get restless again and she must think of something else to keep her quiet. "We can tell stories," she suggested, "or just talk."

"I know what," said Eva, brightening at the thought. "Let's talk about Uncle Jim Bowie. We haven't talked about him for a long time."

"Who's Uncle Bowie?" asked Bena.

Eva pretended to be shocked by her sister's ignorance. "Why, he's your own great-great uncle," she announced proudly. "His sister, Mary, was Mamma's grandmother, and he was an ever so famous man. He was in all kinds of fights . . . and invented a new kind of knife . . . and killed just lots of men!"

"But he was good," interrupted Petite, seeing the look of dismay in Bena's eyes. "He was a good, brave man and he never killed anybody unless he had to. Isn't that right, Mamma?"

"That's right," agreed Mamma. "Only when it was necessary to keep from being killed himself. Life was hard and rough in those days, and men had to know how to protect themselves."

"And when he died in the Alamo," Petite continued, "he gave his life fighting someone else's battle, just because he believed that what they were fighting for was right." She went on to tell several well-known Bowie stories, taking care to include all the exciting details to entertain her little sisters.

Sugar Petite

But Eva was still pursuing her own level of thought. "I wonder if he went to heaven?" she mused. "After killing all those people, I mean."

"Of course he did," Petite answered emphatically. "He wouldn't be kept out of heaven for something he couldn't help."

"Well, I do hope you're right. I sure want to see him up there someday. There are so many things I'd like to ask him."

They all fell silent a moment, trying to picture the future interview between Eva and her famous kinsman; and as they did, they noticed that the sound both of the wind and the rain had almost ceased.

"Listen," said Petite. "Listen, Mamma, the wind has died down and the rain is just a gentle patter!"

They listened, and marvelled that the frightening sounds of a short time ago could so suddenly change into the friendly, almost playful, little pit-a-pat they now heard.

Mamma's soft voice was warm and happy again. "I've often thought," she said, "that the gentle rain so often following a bad storm is like an ashamed little child after a temper tantrum, trying to show the world how sweet and good he can really be."

It was still almost as dark as before, but fear had departed on the wings of the storm. The little group inside the shelter lay quiet and relaxed, listening to the penitent voice of the rain drops.

And suddenly, there was Papa calling through the semi-darkness: "Hallo! Anybody at home in there?"

The Hurricane

His face appeared at the round end of the tunnel. "The old house weathered the storm, and I'm lonesome for my family."

14. The Gypsies

As long as she lived, Petite would remember the day of the gypsies' visit. Almost always the gypsies came in the springtime, camping for several weeks somewhere along the side of the road between Belle Vale and the levee, usually close to the plantation store where they were conveniently located to do the bit of trading which was their only apparent means of livelihood. There were never many of them—two or three families at most—strange, dark looking people who travelled in covered wagons, wore odd, bright-colored clothes, spoke with an unfamiliar accent, and cooked their meals in the open while their horses grazed on the thick grass that carpeted the levee.

The children at Belle Vale were never allowed too close a look at them, but occasionally they saw them from the windows of the carriage or buggy when they were lucky enough to be passing by at the right time. Then they always craned their necks to take in as many details as possible during those few precious moments. Later they compared notes on what they had seen—bright silk scarves and rugs, colored beads and other trinkets, and carved wooden objects—all displayed for sale; and sometimes a gypsy woman reading the palm of one of the colored folk, who couldn't resist the temptation of having their fortunes told.

Always when the gypsies were in the neighborhood, an atmosphere of excitement and suspense hung over the plantation. Doors were kept carefully closed, and colored nurses were instructed to keep a watchful eye on their

The Gypsies

little charges. For gypsies were supposed to steal children and, although no one could remember an actual case of its having happened, there was always the chance that this year might prove the truth behind the tradition. The older children were forbidden to play far from the house, and the younger ones were kept within arm's reach of their protective nursemaids.

However, if uneasiness reigned during the gypsies' stay, there was also a feeling of concern when, as it very rarely happened, they failed to make an appearance at the usual time. If, one year, April should turn into May and May into June without the arrival of the familiar covered wagons, in awed tones the word would spread from cabin to cabin and finally to the big house: "The gypsies didn't come this year. The gypsies didn't come!" No one seemed to stop to reason that perhaps they had simply chosen a different spot for their spring camping-ground. To everyone it seemed that nature's plan had somehow been mysteriously interrupted, as surely as if the robins had failed to come, or the trees to clothe themselves in green, or the dogwood to bloom in soft, white clouds throughout the countryside. And not until the next year, when the anxiously awaited news spread through the plantation: "The gypsies are back! They've come again!" did everyone breathe easily once more and rest assured that the rightful order of things had been fully restored.

Yet, as familiar a part of springtime as the gypsies were at Belle Vale, they never approached the house. They seemed content to stay close to their wagons, living their own strange lives, with no more contact with the rest of the world than was absolutely necessary.

It was, therefore, with a start of surprise that Petite

Sugar Petite

saw the group approaching the back door. She had gone out on the porch to get some butter for "Aunt Rachel" with whom she was visiting in the kitchen, and she was just emerging from the dairy safe with a jar in her hand when she heard the sound of voices and footsteps outside. Coming toward the back steps were a man, a woman, and a little girl about five or six years old. The woman and child wore bright skirts and blouses, with several strands of beads around their necks. Their dark hair hung around their shoulders, and on their arms they each carried a large basket. Unmistakably, they were gypsies!

Petite darted through the kitchen door, dumping the butter in front of startled "Aunt Rachel," to whom she uttered the single word: "Gypsies!" as she rushed into the house in search of Papa.

It was a late Saturday morning, and she found him at his desk where he was going over his account books as he always did after paying the plantation help. Petite blurted out the news she had to tell him: "The gypsies are here, right at the back door! Come quickly, Papa, the gypsies!"

He closed the book very quietly and pushed the chair back from his desk. She wondered how he could be so calm. He didn't even hurry as he walked through the hall, while she fairly danced with excitement at his side. By the time they reached the porch, "Aunt Rachel" was talking to the gypsies through the back door. Clearly she was taking no chances by letting them in.

"Dey wants to buy some veg'tables from de gahden," she informed them as they joined the group.

"Good morning," said Papa politely.

The man, who answered in broken English, gestured

The Gypsies

broadly with his hands as he spoke. "We like ze greens —fraish greens from ze gardain. For ze cheeldren." He pointed to the little girl. "Ze cheeldren need ze greens. We have monies to pay." He motioned to the woman, who promptly held out a small, brightly beaded purse which she shook to produce a convincing, jingling sound.

But Papa wasn't looking at either of them. His eyes were fixed on the little girl who stood shyly clinging to her mother's skirt. She was, Petite decided, one of the prettiest little girls she had ever seen. She had enormous, almond-shaped eyes fringed with dark lashes; and her long, thick hair framed a delicate, oval shaped face of such perfection that she looked more like a doll than a real child. To be sure, she appeared in need of a good bath, as well as a comb and brush, but even the dirt could not hide the fact that she was an unusual little beauty.

"You may have the greens," said Papa, "and you may keep the money. You are welcome to all you can pick and carry off yourselves. I'll walk to the garden with you." He turned to Petite. "You want to come, too, Sugar? Maybe you'd like to help the little girl with the picking. Her hands don't look very big."

For the next half-hour they gathered vegetables in the garden. After the mustard greens, Papa invited them to pick some of the green beans that hung so invitingly on the vines nearby. Then, when Petite pulled a carrot to show to the child and he saw the delighted smile that brightened her serious little face, he suggested that they also take along a supply of these.

Finally the three baskets were filled to the brim. As the gypsy man thanked Papa for his kindness, the woman turned to Petite. "You good to us," she said

Sugar Petite

with a smile that made her face almost as pretty as her little daughter's. "I like to be good to you. You come to our wagons—I tell you ze future . . ."

"Oh, Papa, could I?" begged Petite, her heart already pounding with excitement at the thought. "If you or Jimmie went with me, could I go this afternoon . . . please?"

Papa hesitated a minute. Then, "I don't see why not," he decided, "since our friends are kind enough to ask you."

Petite thought of Eva, who was playing with Indie and the younger children near the stable and was missing all this wonderful experience. If only she could go, too! "I have a sister," she ventured boldly.

Papa frowned, but the gypsy woman nodded her head. "She come, too," she said. "Everybody come. Everybody have a future!"

As they watched them leave, Papa took Petite by the arm. "We'll never have any trouble with the gypsies," he said. "There goes our insurance. Remember this always, Sugar. Sometimes a single gesture of kindness can be the best insurance in the world."

That afternoon, Jimmie went with the girls to the gypsy camp. They decided to walk because it was such a beautiful late spring day. The sky was clear and blue, and although the warmth of the sunlight was already giving warning of the hot days ahead, a cool breeze from the river fanned and refreshed them as they walked along the travel-worn road.

This had been the most wonderful spring Petite had ever known. It wasn't just the things that had happened. The visit to Pinkie's cabin in the middle of the night, the hurricane, and now the gypsies' visit—all these events

The Gypsies
were exciting, it was true; but life at Belle Vale always held its share of excitement.

And it wasn't anything about the springtime itself. After the hurricane, the plantation had been set in order again, with everyone working together to pick up the moss, dead wood and other debris that had been blown about; and the colored men mending fences and repairing shingles on the roofs. Then the days had once more pursued their usual uninterrupted course.

There had been the familiar succession of spring flowers—dainty "snowdrops" and blue phlox, followed by the great red flowers of amaryllis, large white iris, and flaming patches of "burning bush" with their bright, oriental looking blossoms bursting along slim, brown stems. One by one the birds had returned to Belle Vale, the same little friends that were welcomed every spring— the tiny humming birds, swooping night-hawks and darting chimney swifts, bright summer tanigers and indigo buntings, the liquid voiced wood thrush—all added their quick flashes of plummage and movement to the garden and, because of their winter absence, seemed more dear than the mockingbirds, blue jays, cardinals and other birds that remained throughout the winter months.

The usual round of spring activities had taken place, including the planting of the cane crop and vegetable garden and the arrival of new calves and piglets. The winter rainwater, collected during the cold months from the well-scrubbed gutters, had been run from the two wooden cisterns into iron tanks under the house, to be used as drinking water during the summer when dust and insects would make fresh rainwater unsafe. In the yard, the huge iron smudge pots, another of Papa's favorite precautions, had been made ready to be filled

Sugar Petite

with burning tar and sawdust at the sign of the first hungry mosquito. In the kitchen, also, the signs of spring were the same as always—fresh vegetables and strawberries prepared by Aunt Rachel's ever busy fingers; and crawfish heads, stuffed with savory dressing, ready to be dropped into the dark, thick bisque.

Dr. Stocking had made his annual visit, setting up his dental office in the parlor and staying as a guest at the house until every tooth in the family was put into excellent shape.

No, Petite decided, this springtime really hadn't been different from any other. The difference lay, somehow, within herself; in the way she felt. No longer were there the comfortable inbetween shades of perception that she had always known—the hazy meeting ground of good and evil, beauty and ugliness, joy and sorrow, that had allowed her to be aware of and, at the same time, disregard them. All at once, a beautiful sight, a piece of music, or a poem seemed to fill her heart to overflowing and bring tears to her eyes; while an act of unkindness or story of cruelty left her either angry or afraid. This year when she found a dead baby bird fallen from its nest, as the children so often did in the early spring, she suddenly felt like bursting into tears and had fled to the security of her room, away from the curious eyes of her playmates. She knew that she was crying, not only for the little bird that would never know the joy of winging its way through the bright air, but also for all the ugliness and cruelty that was a part of the world and that she would never be able to change. And yet she felt, mixed with her tears, a new sense of gladness because she realized that she was sharing more deeply in life's experiences than she ever had before.

The Gypsies

Strange as her new depths of joy and sorrow seemed to her, there was another sensation that was even stranger. She had felt it first one night while she was sitting alone on the gallery steps after supper, watching the shadows of the moss-hung trees in the moonlight. All at once her heart had begun to beat very fast and she had had the distinct feeling that something very wonderful was about to happen. She couldn't tell what it was, but suddenly it had seemed to her that the night and the moon and the swaying strands of moss were all trying to tell her something, some beautiful secret meant only for her.

Since then, she had had the feeling many times—a sort of breathless waiting for something to happen—and often she had slipped alone onto the moonlit gallery to listen to the secrets of the night. Once she had decided to ask Papa about it, reasoning quite sensibly that perhaps other people felt that way, too. But when he looked up from his book in the parlor, she had found herself feeling hesitant and foolish, and had crept away with her question still unasked . . .

Today, however, there was no doubt as to the reason for her feeling of anticipation. In the distance before them, they could already see the wagons and tents of the gypsy camp.

"I'm s'prised Papa let us come," said Eva, as the two girls hurried along, taking several short steps to each of Jimmie's long ones. "I thought fortune telling was wicked."

"Not if you don't really believe in it," answered Petite. "We're just going for fun, and so as not to hurt the gypsies' feelings. But we're not to take seriously anything they tell us; Papa said so. And we're not to go in the

Sugar Petite

wagons or tents; and if they offer us anything to eat, we can take it to be polite, but not eat it—just pretend we want to take it home."

"So many *don'ts* drown out the *do's*," commented Eva. "But, anyway, I'm glad we're getting to go."

There were only two wagons this year, and Petite immediately recognized their friends near the first of them. The man was not in sight; but the woman was there, cooking something in a big, black pot hung over an open fire. Seated on the ground, the little girl was playing with a dirty, black and white puppy. She jumped up when she saw them coming and ran to hide behind her mother's skirts. The little dog began barking at them in short, shrill yelps.

"Hush, 'Cheeta'," said the gypsy woman, coming forward to welcome them. She kicked lightly at the puppy and sent it yiping from the scene. "Your fortune, young ladies?" She held out her brown hand after greeting the group. "I mus' study ze palm to tell what ze future hold. One at a time, please."

Eva promptly shot forward her chubby hand, at the same time deluging the gypsy with a flood of questions: "Am I gonna be pretty when I'm grown? And am I gonna be rich? Am I gonna get married? And how many children will I have?"

134

The Gypsies

The fortune teller looked somewhat taken aback; but she calmly placed Eva's hand, palm upward, upon her own and carefully studied its lines.

"I see a beautiful young ladee and a mos' handsome young man," she said dreamily, and smiled at the dreamy look that immediately came over Eva's face. "I see a fine wedding. I see a large home. I see servants and many pretty clothes. I see . . ."

"I hope you don't see too many children," volunteered Eva. "It's so hard to keep up with 'em and make 'em behave."

The gypsy hesitated, closed Eva's hand, and studied the creases beneath her little finger. Then, "I see two pretty cheeldren—a boy and a girl."

"Good," said Eva, beaming with joy. "Everything just the way I want it!"

With Eva so perfectly satisfied, there was no need to continue with her fortune, and the gypsy turned to Petite. She looked long and hard into her eyes, something she hadn't done with Eva. Petite thought she had never seen such eyes—so large and dark that for a moment she had the frightening feeling that she was going to be drawn right into them and lost in their depths. Then the gypsy looked at her palm, studying it silently as she traced the lines with one finger.

"I see a long life, a happy life, a life of loving othairs and making zem happy. I see a time away from home, a time at home again, and then away—but not far. I see cheeldren.—" She studied the hand again. "I see grand-cheeldren and . . . yes, great-grandcheeldren."

"Oh, my goodness," exclaimed Petite. "That's enough! Let's not go any farther than that!" The prediction of

Sugar Petite

great-grandchildren was entirely more than she had bargained for.

The woman closed her hand but still kept it within her own. "Ze palm tell only your own future," she said, "but I can see othair theengs—" She closed her eyes and began swaying gently back and forth: "I see new happiness in ze beeg house. I hear a baby cry. I see a young lady change her home but not her name. I see a leetle girl become a woman and fall een love . . ."

Petite pulled her hand away and turned to Jimmie. She felt a little frightened and didn't want to hear any more. "You now, Jimmie," she said. "You take your turn."

But Jimmie refused. "I just came with you girls," he muttered. Petite could tell he wasn't very much impressed with the fortunes he had just heard.

Before they left, the gypsy mother made her little girl sing and dance for them. Reluctant at first, she danced very gracefully once she had begun, accompanying her quick steps with a wild sounding song in some foreign language. Jimmie handed each of the girls a coin to give to her. He had been instructed by Papa not to pay the woman for the fortune telling, since they had come at her bidding which was a gesture of thanks for the vegetables.

As the three walked homeward in the lengthening shadows, Eva remarked disappointedly, "She didn't give us anything to eat, after all."

"Well, I'm glad she didn't," said Petite, " 'cause Papa would have made us throw it away. Anyhow, whatever she was cooking in that pot smelled just awful. I'm sort of glad to be going home."

"I think it was all simply wonderful," Eva said. "Just

The Gypsies

think, I'm going to have a rich husband and only two children!"

"Papa told us not to believe anything she said," Petite reminded her. But she, too, fell to wondering over some of the gypsy's words.

. . . . .

That night, Carrie looked up from her sewing as Petite tiptoed cautiously through the hall and into the parlor. The single oil lamp, burning on the table beside her, cast a bright light only in the end of the room where she was working and threw deep shadows into the distant corners.

"What's the matter, honey? Can't you go to sleep?"

"No, I can't," said Petite, "It's lonesome in there without you, and I keep thinking about the gypsies."

She sat down on the sofa beside her sister. The horsehair under the black upholstery pricked through her nightdress, and she got up to find a newspaper on which to sit before settling herself again.

Carrie moved over to give her more room. "Papa will be sorry he let you go if he thinks it upset you. What is it that's bothering you? Something she told you about your future?"

"Oh, it's not exactly bothering me. Everything she said sounded real nice. It's just that I don't understand how she knew the things she did. Of course, with Eva all she had to do was answer her questions the way she knew she wanted her to. I figured that out right away. But how did she know . . . Carrie, how did she know Mamma's going to have another baby?"

Carrie looked up in surprise. "Did she say that?"

"Well, not exactly. She said, 'I see new happiness in

Sugar Petite

the big house. I hear a baby cry.' What else could she have meant?"

"Did *you* know about it before?" Carrie asked quietly. Having babies was not a subject for general discussion, and she wasn't sure how much her little sister knew.

"Well, I sort of suspected it the day of the hurricane when Papa told me to take care of Mamma for him, and then—well, lately I've been pretty sure. You see, I remember before Nootsie was born."

Carrie laid down her sewing and smiled at her. "Well, it's true," she said, "and isn't it fun to think of having another tiny baby in the house?" Petite agreed, although she couldn't see that a tiny baby was much of a novelty in their family. "As for the gypsies," Carrie went on, "finding out news is a big part of their business. They have ways of picking up bits of neighborhood gossip wherever they are—this time probably from some of the colored folk—and then they pass it off as something they know through a magic power of their own."

"Oh," said Petite, feeling a trifle disappointed . . . "What are you making?" She reached over and fingered the soft, white material on which Carrie was sewing. Already it showed hours of patient work, with fine stitching, tucks and embroidery.

"It's a corset cover. Isn't it going to be pretty?"

"A *corset cover!* Why in the world are you putting all that work on a corset cover? All that fancy sewing on something nobody'll ever see!"

"I thought I'd like one real pretty one," said Carrie. She tried to sound matter of fact, but her cheeks turned red and she kept her eyes on her work as she spoke.

Suddenly the truth of another of the gypsy's predictions burst upon Petite. *"I see a young lady change her*

The Gypsies
home but not her name," she had said. For some months now, Carrie had been keeping company with a young gentleman from across the river in West Feliciana Parish, a very distant cousin who had the same name as theirs. Carrie was going to marry John—and she was sewing on her trousseau! He was going to see her in this very corset cover!

At first the thought seemed so utterly scandalous, she gulped and felt her own cheeks grow red. The next instant, she was kneeling on the floor in front of her big sister. Another wedding in the family! Another bride and groom repeating their marriage vows before the flower-banked parlor mantel and later greeting all the neighbors and friends who would be there to wish them happiness. This was really exciting news!

She circled her arms around Carrie's knees and looked up at her. "You're going to get married, aren't you?" she asked softly and then, without waiting for an answer, "Why haven't you told me about it?"

Carrie smiled. "I was going to tell you before long," she said. "It's still such a long way off, probably late in the fall, so we're waiting awhile to tell anyone. I don't think there should be too much excitement right now, on account of Mamma . . . and, of course, I want to be at home until after the baby comes and everything is running smoothly again."

How like Carrie to be thinking of everyone else before herself! What would they do when she was gone?

"I don't want you to leave home," said Petite. "Nothing will ever seem right without you."

Carrie stroked her hair. "And I don't want to leave any of you, but there comes a time . . . Anyway, I'll be living just across the river. We can see each other often."

Sugar Petite

Petite hadn't meant to tell her the other part of the gypsy's fortune, but all at once the moment seemed just right. "The gypsy said she saw a little girl becoming a woman and falling in love. Do you s'pose she meant me?"

Carrie laughed. "I'm sure she did," she said, "but that was a pretty safe thing for her to foretell. With all the little girls around here, there's bound to be a lot of growing up and falling in love some day."

"I don't *ever* want to fall in love," Petite said emphatically, "unless I can find someone just like Papa—just like him without his beard, of course. I can't imagine Papa without his, but I don't believe I'd want to marry a man with a beard."

Carrie laughed again, this time at the thought of Petite with a bearded husband. Then she became serious once more. "I used to feel that way, too, until I met John," she said, "and it's strange but, in most ways, he's not at all like Papa. It seems to be something you can't know in advance or really understand when it comes. The chances are that the man you fall in love with someday won't be like Papa either."

"Maybe not," said Petite without enthusiasm, "but it'll sure be a surprise to me!" She decided not to tell Carrie about the great-grandchildren.

15. *New Happiness in the Big House*

"I wonder what it's like to have a baby—" She didn't word it like a question but, quite intentionally, there was a note of question in her voice. If Julia noticed, however, she paid no attention. She shifted her position on the step on which they were sitting and frowned at her companion.

"Yo' papa'd be mighty mad if he knowed you's settin' here. He tole you to go to sleep upstairs, an' you's purely disobeyin' him, dat's what!"

Petite returned her frown. "I'm not disobeying him at all," she whispered. "He told me to sleep upstairs, but he didn't say *when*, and I'm not sleepy. Anyway, I *am* upstairs. I'm on the top step!"

Downstairs in her bedroom, behind carefully closed doors, Mamma was having her baby. No one had told Petite this, but she knew it without the telling. A little while after supper, Papa had informed the children that they were all to sleep upstairs tonight; that they could have a "house party" in the two bedrooms up there, and wouldn't that be fun? They were to get their things without bothering Mamma, who wasn't feeling very well. Julia had helped them gather up their night clothes, and he had gone upstairs with them to see that they were all properly settled—Eva and Petite in the Guest Room, and Bena and Nootsie in the Boys' Room with a mattress on the floor for Julia. Nootsie was already sleepy; and Papa had stayed to tuck him in, after pushing one of the beds against the wall and placing two chairs on the open side to keep him from falling out.

Sugar Petite

You'll have to sleep in a big bed now," he had said as he kissed him goodnight. "Nootsie must learn to be a big boy."

"Big boy! Nootsie big boy!" It was a happy, sleepy little voice that answered him; and as he stood there for a moment looking down at his small son, there had been a thoughtful, almost sad expression on his face. Petite had felt a lump rise in her throat, and tears that stung at the back of her eyes. This was the last night that Nootsie would be the baby in the family. Tomorrow he must become one of the older children and grow accustomed to seeing another little baby in the place he knew and loved so well. Would the sudden change be hard for him? She must remember to spend extra time with him during the next few weeks and try to help him over this first hard bump in his very young life.

If Eva suspected anything out of the ordinary, she had kept it locked within herself. She was delighted with the idea of spending the night in the Guest Room and had put on such a show of grownup airs as she made ready for bed that Petite had been forced to bite her lip to keep from making unkind remarks. Petite had undressed, too, and had stayed in bed with her little sister, doing her patient best to keep up with her gay, foolish chatter until sleep finally overcame her and a peaceful quiet settled over the shuttered room. Then she had slipped out of bed and, carrying her pillow with her, had tiptoed through the hall to take her place at the top of the stairs.

It was quiet in the other bedroom, too, and she had hoped that Julia hadn't heard her; but the alert little colored maid, with the well-trained ear of a children's nurse, had soon joined her on the steps. She had no

New Happiness in the Big House

patience with Petite's plea that she couldn't go to sleep. To her, obedience was obedience when her master spoke, and could not be altered by fine interpretation of words or circumstance. And yet, a feeling of loyalty to her little mistress kept her at her side in the dimly lighted hall.

Seeing that no other method was going to succeed, Petite decided to abandon subtlety in favor of a direct question: "Julia, what's it like having a baby?"

She knew that Julia could tell her if she would. All colored people knew about having babies, with new arrivals in the cabins at very frequent intervals; and although Julia had lived with the white family since early childhood, she had spent enough time in "the quarters" to be well versed in all their ways.

Julia looked at her steadily, in seemingly endless silence. "Well," she said at last, "it's like nothin' else in de whole wide world 'cept jes' having a baby. You jes' has it, dat's all!" She closed her lips again in a determined line.

"*Well, what a help!*" thought Petite. "*So now I know!*"

Really, of course, she knew practically nothing. Down in the parlor she could hear Papa talking and laughing with Dr. Randolph, who had arrived about an hour ago. Steve had gone for Mrs. Broussard and, immediately upon arrival, she had shut herself up in the room with Mamma. Carrie was busying herself with little errands in and out of the room and was keeping the parlor supplied with hot coffee. Petite was glad that the landing and the turn of the stairway made her invisible from downstairs. Here she could remain unseen in the shadows and, at the same time, keep at least partly aware of what was going on below.

Sugar Petite

She knew that Mrs. Broussard was called a "midwife" and that it was her business in life to help ladies have their babies. But why she was called by that strange name, or just what she did to help, Petite had not the faintest idea. It was all a part of that hushed subject about which little girls were not supposed to ask any questions.

"Will Dr. Randolph be with Mamma when she has the baby?" she ventured cautiously.

Julia looked shocked. "Of co'se not," she answered emphatically. "Now, Petite, you know better'n dat! You know it wouldn' be propah fo' some gentleman not even kin to yo' mamma to be in de same room wif her whilse she's havin' a baby! Miz Broussard ten' to all dat—"

"*All what?*" thought Petite, feeling a small flicker of anger flare up within her. Why should Papa and Dr. Randolph stay in the parlor, enjoying themselves and drinking coffee when they might be doing something useful?

"Well, why is the doctor here at all then?" she asked.

"Dat's jes' de way dey does it," said Julia. "Aftah de baby come, he'll go in an' see is it an' yo' mamma all right."

"Why shouldn't she be all right?" The small flicker of anger turned suddenly to one of fright and leaped into a bright flame. "Why did you say that, Julia?"

"Oh, I was jes' talkin'," Julia replied vaguely. "Now listen, Petite, yo' mamma's goin' to git along jes' fine. Look at all de babies she's done had already! Why, by dis time she don't hahdly think nothin' at all 'bout havin' one."

Petite relaxed. Julia was right. This was Mamma's

New Happiness in the Big House

tenth baby, which meant that she must be pretty expert at it by now. *"Practice makes perfect,"* she reminded herself. She thought of her piano lessons and the hours she had spent carefully going over each piece until she could play it without even looking at the music. Surely Mamma had had enough practice.

Once more, however, the thought of Dr. Randolph waiting all this time across the hall, the lateness of the hour, and the bewildering uncertainty of everything that was happening combined into a great fear that welled up within her.

"Julia," she wailed suddenly. "Go get Papa—I want to talk to him!"

"Go git yo' papa?" Julia repeated incredulously. "Me go in dere an' git him? No, ma'am, Petite. Ah cain't do dat! He'd— he'd— No, ma'am, I jes' cain't!"

"You can do what I tell you!" Petite said harshly and realized, with tears in her eyes, that for the first time in her life she had used a tone of command in addressing Julia. Without another word the colored girl arose and crept down the stairs.

By the time she returned with Papa, Petite had worked herself into a high state of runaway emotions. She was worried about Mamma, she had spoken unkindly to Julia, and her conscience was bothering her for having disobeyed her father. It was probably the sight of her tears that kept him from being angry. He stood above her in the semi-darkness, his arm resting lightly on the stair rail. "What are you doing here?" he asked, but his voice was gentle and full of understanding.

"I'm worried about Mamma . . ."

"I told you to go to bed upstairs."

"But I'm not sleepy. How can I be sleepy, Papa, with

Sugar Petite

Mamma down there having a baby? And anyway, I don't like having to stay upstairs with the little children. Carrie doesn't have to stay and . . . and I'm not *really* a little girl any more. Mamma was just three years older than I am when she had Brother Johnny. I don't *like* being treated like a baby myself!"

She stopped, surprised at her own words, and felt, rather than really saw, the surprised look on Papa's face.

"I want you to tell me about her," she went on. "Are you sure she's all right?"

Papa laughed. He sat down on the step below her, taking her hand in his. "Of course she's all right," he said with both pride and confidence reflected in his voice. "You know, Sugar, your mother is good at doing lots of things, but the thing she does the very best of all is having fine, beautiful little babies! She's already proved that, hasn't she?"

Her heart gave a comfortable skip back to normal as her feeling of concern changed to one of happy excitement. After a moment of silence she asked: "Do you think it'll be a boy or a girl. Which would you rather have?"

"You know, it really doesn't matter in the least," he replied. "Not the least bit in the world. Of course, this family could use another boy, and a little brother would be fun for Nootsie. But with my girls all growing up so fast," he gave her hand a hard squeeze, "I'd be mighty glad to have another little girl to take the place of the one just now growing up."

As she hung her head, feeling both happy and confused, he went on: "Now, I'll make a bargain with you. You go on to bed and promise to stay there, and I'll promise to come wake you just as soon as the baby is

New Happiness in the Big House

born. How will that be? You can see it before any of the other children. I'm sure your mother would want it that way."

Petite stood up. Her back was aching, and her eyes were suddenly heavy with sleep. "All right," she agreed, "but don't you dare forget! Come on, Julia." She was careful to make her voice sound kindly. She wanted to say that she was sorry for the way she had spoken a few moments before, but she didn't know how to word it. "Come on, let's get some sleep."

Hours later, she awoke to find Papa shaking her gently by the arm. "Wake up, Petite," he whispered. "The baby has come. You have a new little sister, and Mamma wants you to come down to see her."

She sat up, rubbing her eyes as she struggled back to consciousness. Her father was holding a candle that cast a flickering light on the big bed where Eva was still sleeping soundly beside her. Suddenly, as she realized what was happening, she jumped to the floor, reaching for the dressing gown she had laid out in readiness before going to sleep.

"How's Mamma?" she asked softly as they tiptoed together down the stairs.

"Oh, she's just fine," he reassured her, "and so is the baby. We've named her Jenny Lydia, and she's as pretty as a picture. You're going to love her."

Halfway down the steps, Petite stopped and stood still, listening to the sound coming from Mamma and Papa's room. She had never thought that the sound of crying could be so strange and beautiful, like music that made her heart feel full of joy and wonder. Papa turned and smiled at her . . .

Sugar Petite

"*I see new happiness in the big house,*" the gypsy had said. "*I hear a baby cry. I see a little girl become a woman—*"

Upstairs the younger children were all fast asleep. But she was going to join the grownups, to welcome the tiny new member of the family.

16. Petite Meets Charlie

"Clippety-clop, clippety-clop." The turning of the wheels and the beat of the horses' hooves joined in gay rhythm as the carriage rolled along the road beside the levee.

Petite sat straight against the leather upholstery. She held her head high, trying to look as old as Lena sitting opposite her. When brother Jimmie smiled at her, she lowered her eyes and smoothed out the folds of the white dress she was wearing. It was the dress that Carrie had helped her make, and she was proud of the way it had turned out. It fitted just right, with exactly the proper number of darts at the waistline to flatter the new young lady figure she was finally beginning to realize was her own.

It was mid-summer, a wonderful summer she would never forget—with Lena home from school bringing so many exciting things to talk about; the plans for Carrie's wedding to discuss; the new baby to love and fondle; the sunsets more beautiful and the blackberries, watermelons and river shrimp more delicious than she had ever known before. The days were slipping by too quickly. If only there could be some way to hold them back and make them last forever!

Outside the carriage window, the countryside sailed past them in the moonlight. For a moment she was reminded of the time she and Papa had gone to see Pinkie when he was sick, but then she realized how great a difference there was tonight. They were going to a dance; and she was to make her first appearance as a

Sugar Petite

real young lady, with her dress as long as grownups, her hair piled high on top of her head, and real jewelry like all the other ladies would be wearing. She reached up and felt the dainty gold pendants hanging from her ears. They were really Carrie's, lent to her for the occasion; but somehow this seemed to give her added confidence, as if the earrings, at least, had had some experience at grownup parties and would therefore manage to guide her through the evening and see that she didn't do anything wrong.

She wished that Mamma and Papa could be with them, but they had said that little Jenny was still too young for them to leave. Carrie had gone in the buggy with her John, and brother Jimmie had good naturedly consented to escort his two younger sisters. It gave her a grand, important feeling to be riding in the carriage at night, with Steve holding the reins up front and "Molly" and "Stockings" trotting along so smoothly it almost seemed that they must know what an important event this was for her. It made her think of Cinderella going to the ball in her magic pumpkin carriage, but she immediately dismissed this thought as being too childish to go with her long, white dress.

About six miles down the road beyond Port Allen was the little settlement of Back Brusly where, in a large old building known as Doiron Hall, the neighboring plantation families gathered from time to time for dances and other entertainments. Petite had been there before, to parties when whole families were invited—children as well as grownups. And once, when she was very little, she had taken part in a Christmas play produced by the combined efforts of the community for the benefit of some charitable cause. She had been cast as an angel in

Petite Meets Charlie

a filmy costume complete with wings and, seated on a swing suspended from the roof by long ropes, she had sailed high above the heads of the admiring audience. Sometimes she still dreamed about it at night and again felt herself flying through the air, with many faces turned upward to look at her. But to a real dance she had never been. Other people sometimes took their children, but Papa always refused with the same remark—a remark that had something to do with there being "a time and a place."

"What's the first thing we do when we get there?" she asked. "I mean just as soon as we step inside the door?"

"Well, first we'll go and speak to the hosts and hostesses," her brother informed her, "and then I'll take turns dancing with you girls . . . unless, of course, you'd like to try it at the same time. I'm not sure, but I believe I could swing the two of you together." The girls giggled. "Really, though, I'm counting on each of you catching a beau for yourself at the first possible moment. I'm making no promises about sticking around if another pretty girl happens to catch my eye!"

"Now, Jimmie, don't tease," begged Petite. "I won't care if I don't get to dance at all. I'm sure there'll be lots of people I know, and I can sit with them and watch. I believe I'd rather just watch a while, anyway, until I kind of catch on what to do."

Once there, however, it was easy to become a part of the party in progress. At one end of the brightly lighted hall, an orchestra seated on a platform was playing wonderful, gay sounding music; at the other end, a festively decorated table held a large silver bowl of punch, and trays of delicious cakes and cookies. Along the two side walls there were chairs for those who didn't care to dance.

Sugar Petite

On one of these chairs Petite promptly placed herself while Jimmie danced first with Lena. Next to her were seated some friends of her parents whom she had known since she was a little girl. They commented with enthusiasm on the way she had grown up during the summer and what a pretty young lady she had turned out to be, to which she replied modestly, wondering all the while if the hairpins were staying in place. Mamma had warned her against feeling to see, saying that a young lady of good manners didn't "fiddle" too much with her hair or dress. Carrie and John came over and talked with her for a while, as did several young people she knew from neighboring plantations. The rest of the time she just sat watching the dancers and enjoying the music and laughter all around her.

All at once, she had the uneasy feeling that someone was watching her. It was a funny little sensation that sent tingles to the back of her neck. Slowly she let her eyes wander around the hall and, sure enough, standing in a group in one corner, three young men all had their eyes fixed in her direction. One of them seemed to be questioning the others, who were nodding in reply while looking straight at her.

She lowered her head, gazing demurely at her hands folded in her lap. Was it possible that they were really looking at her? If so, surely they wouldn't dare come near—or would they? She thought of Mamma and Papa and the children, safe at home. Almost she wished . . .

When she looked up again, Lena was dancing with someone else, and coming toward her were Jimmie and one of the young men who had attracted her attention. Jimmie had him by the arm and was talking easily with him. On his face he wore an amused expression.

Petite Meets Charlie

"Petite," he said formally as they drew near, "may I present a young friend of mine who has asked to be introduced to you? This is . . ."

She didn't even hear the name, she was so busy concentrating on how she should reply. "How do you do?" she said primly, bending her head to a carefully calculated angle.

Then she looked at him and as she did, her heart gave a leap. He had black, wavy hair; a round face with a strong, determined looking chin; and dark eyes that held a certain kindly twinkle she had seen before. *"He looks just like Papa,"* she thought with a kind of desperate unbelief. *"He's just the way Papa must have looked when he was young, before he grew a beard!"*

His name was Charlie. He lived across the river in Baton Rouge and had come over for a visit with friends, in order to attend the dance. His family knew hers, and he had met Jimmie while the latter was going to L.S.U. He had been off to school in Bell Buckle, Tennessee, and would have another year up there before graduating from high school in the spring.

He wasn't very tall, Petite noticed when they started in to dance; but, even so, he was comfortably taller than she. He was straight and slim, but a certain square set to his shoulders made her think that someday even his build might be like her father's.

It didn't take her long to discover that he wasn't a good dancer. He stepped several times on her toes, apologized, and finally gave up with a laugh. "Let's go get some punch," he suggested, "before I ruin your poor feet beyond repair. I'm afraid I've neglected my dancing lessons."

The night was very warm, and the punch tasted

Sugar Petite

delicious. He carried her cup for her as they went over to sit at the side of the room.

"Do you think practice might help?" he asked as they seated themselves.

"Practice? Oh, you mean your dancing? Well, that wasn't really all your fault, you know. I've never had much practice myself. My sisters and I dance together at home, and sometimes brother Jimmie will dance with us but . . ." She hesitated, not sure whether or not she should go on. "This is the first time I've ever been to a real dance."

He looked surprised. "It is? How old are you, anyway? Or shouldn't I ask that question?"

"Oh, that's all right. I'm thirteen." Then she added quickly: "But I'm *almost* fourteen!" Suddenly it seemed a very important thing for him to know.

He smiled. "I would have thought you were even older than that," he added, looking at her with admiration, "but it really doesn't matter. I'm just seventeen myself. And not even *almost* eighteen," he added with a mischievous light in his eyes. "You know what?" He stood up. "It's hot as blazes in here, and lots of people are out on the gallery cooling off. Do you suppose it would be all right for us to go out there, if we spoke to your brother first?"

When they asked him, Jimmie laughingly gave his consent, with a teasing remark about "no dark corners" that made Petite resolve to settle with him when the evening was over. She knew that her cheeks were red, but Charlie just grinned and didn't seem to mind.

All the chairs on the gallery were already taken, but they found a place on the steps. He carefully spread out his handkerchief before she sat down, and she wondered

Petite Meets Charlie
at his thoughtfulness. Most boys wouldn't have noticed that her dress was dainty and white and something to be treated with care.

They fell to talking about themselves. His last name was an Irish one, he told her, and he was very proud of the fact. When his grandfather came to America from the Old Country, he had settled across the river in Bayou Sara where he had owned a store. His own father had studied law and was now a judge. But no law books for him! He wanted to study medicine.

"Medicine?" repeated Petite. "You mean you're going to be a doctor?"

"I certainly am. That's one thing I'm sure of, and nothing can change my mind. Oh, I know it means lots of study ahead of me, and maybe a hard time getting started, but it'll be worth it. I'll tell you something—I think, in our lifetime, the world's going to see perfectly wonderful things happen in the field of medicine, especially in surgery. Why, being able to put people to sleep the way they can now—so they don't feel a thing, mind you—just think of all that doctors may someday be able to do to patch them up inside."

Petite tried hard to concentrate on the wonders he was describing. She had to admit that she didn't find it too pleasant a subject for meditation, but his enthusiasm was enough for them both.

"I get excited just thinking about it," he went on, "and I want to be a part of it all. I wouldn't miss it for the world."

He really talked just like a grown person, she decided. He said he thought there was going to be a big change in the way patients felt toward their doctors; in their willingness to let them help them. She wanted to ask him

Sugar Petite

what he thought about doctors being in the room with ladies to help them have their babies; but she checked herself, horrified that such a thought should even have crossed her mind. It was a strange thing though—she had known him for such a very short time, yet already she felt that she could tell him anything and he would understand.

He asked her about herself. Soon she was telling him all about her family, the plantation, the time she had spent away at school, and the wonderful months since Papa had let her come home.

"Do you think you'll go away next year?" he asked.

"I don't know, but I hope not. You see, I love my family so much, I don't think I'll ever leave them unless they make me—"

"I think you're wrong about that," he answered seriously. "Everyone has to get away from home for awhile, you know, in order to become a real individual—to learn to stand on his own feet and make his own decisions. You've got to be able to face the world some day; and I think the longer you put it off, the harder it gets. Oh, you're homesick for a while, of course—I guess everybody is who comes from a happy home—but after a time you get so interested in everything, you forget all about it. And loving your family has nothing to do with it. You can keep right on loving them and, at the same time, know how happy you're making them because they're proud of you."

Petite didn't answer him. She found that she really didn't have a thing to say.

It was Charlie who finally realized how long they'd been away from the rest of the party. As they stood up to go inside, he said to her: "There's something I want

Petite Meets Charlie

to ask you before we go in. Do you think your parents would mind if I came to see you one day before I go back to school? I could spend the night with my friends over here."

"Of course they wouldn't mind," she answered quickly. "They'd be happy to have you, I know—and I'm sure Mamma would want you to have a meal with us. I do hope you'll come."

She said it quite calmly, but her heart picked up the words and beat them into a wild tatoo: *"I hope . . . I hope . . . Oh, how . . . I hope . . ."*

17. The Fruit Peddler

Very carefully, Petite removed the letter from its envelope and spread it unfolded on her lap. With one finger she traced the first two words: "Dear Betsy."

Off in the distance she could hear the happy voices of the children at play. It must be an exciting game, for Indie's raucous voice could be heard above the shrill squeals of the little ones. But up in the tree house it was quiet and peaceful. She had pulled up the ladder to assure complete privacy. Overhead, a roof of green leaves gave her the feeling of being away and away from the rest of the world.

Charlie had come as he promised he would. One morning, quite early, he had arrived on horseback with the announced intention of spending the day with them if it met with their convenience. With mingled pride and shyness, Petite had introduced him to all the family and noticed with delight how well he seemed to fit into the closely knit family circle. He joked playfully with the younger children, admired the sewing at which Mamma and Carrie were working, conversed quite intelligently with both Papa and Jimmie, and was lavish in his praise of the fine chicken pie dinner served by "Aunt Rachel" and "Aunt Harriet" in honor of his presence.

The Fruit Peddler

In a matter of hours, they had all taken him into their hearts as a close and much loved friend. She learned that his father and Papa knew each other well through the legal profession; and there was much discussion of affairs in Baton Rouge, during which time she sat quietly wishing that they wouldn't find quite so much about which to talk.

But that was only at dinnertime. The rest of the day she had him quite to herself. And what a wonderful time they had, wandering together through the different parts of the plantation grounds and sitting and talking on the gallery, with a delicious picnic supper prepared for them by "Aunt Rachel" in the late afternoon.

Just before he left, he had asked if she would write to him while he was away; and after that, when she had answered promptly that she would, he had ventured another and rather amazing question.

"I don't know what you'll think of me," he had said, "but there's something I want to ask you. Do you mind if I call you *Betsy?*"

"*Betsy?*" The name had sounded strange as she said it, although she had to admit that, when spoken by him, it held a definite catchy charm. "Why *Betsy?*" For a moment she had had the awful feeling that maybe he didn't like her real name.

"Oh, I don't know. It's just a funny idea I've always had. Somehow, I've always thought that one of these days, when I had a girl, her name would be Betsy . . ." He had hesitated for a moment and although she was looking away in confusion, she had felt his brown eyes studying her earnestly. "Don't think I'm too bold," he pleaded. "I suppose it's the Irish in me that makes me

Sugar Petite

know right off when I find something I want; and the Irish, too, that makes me seldom change my mind."

Looking at him then and seeing how serious he was and how much it seemed to mean to him, she hadn't felt shy anymore.

"Why, I think *Betsy* is a lovely name," she had replied, putting her hand to her throat to hide the pulse that was beating at a most unladylike rate of speed. "I don't mind if you want to call me that . . ." After all, she wasn't actually saying that she would be his girl. Maybe he wouldn't mention it again.

All this had happened many days ago. And quite abruptly, the shopping trip to New Orleans that she had been planning with Papa, Carrie and Lena had lost its appeal. She didn't admit the reason but, as the time drew near, she had found herself wanting less and less to leave home. What if Charlie should come again? Or perhaps a letter from him? Now they were gone; and here she was, alone in the tree house, with the feeble excuse of a make-believe headache and the wonderful reward of the letter in her hand.

"*Dear Betsy:*

Perhaps you thought I really wouldn't write to you, but here is the proof that I meant what I said and that I hope many letters will cross the miles between us before I see you again. I know that nine months can be a long time and that much can happen, especially if you, too, go off to school; but until I hear otherwise from you, I'm going to think of you as my girl. The day with you and your family was a wonderful one. I wish there might be another one like it, but the weeks ahead of me . . ."

"Petite! Petite! You up dere?"

Julia's voice brought her back to reality with a start.

The Fruit Peddler

It was filled with an urgent note of distress and was raised to a degree of loudness unlike its owner's usual quiet self.

Petite stuck her head over the side of the tree house and peered below. "What's the matter?" she asked.

Julia was standing there, wringing her hands and looking very frightened. "It's dat fruit peddler," she said. "Dat turrible, sneaky one what sold de face cream to Eva. Yo' mamma's takin' a nap wif de baby, an' no one else's in de house, an' Ah don't know should Ah wake her!"

"No, don't wake her," said Petite. "I'll come down." She hastily tucked the letter in the front of her dress and, throwing the ladder over the side of the tree house, began the awkward descent to the ground.

"Where is he?" she asked as she joined Julia.

"Dat's what worryin' me. He was at de front doh, an' Ah tole him to wait dere a minute but . . . but Ah don't see him nowheres now!"

"I guess he went around back," Petite decided. "That's where he should have gone in the first place."

Together they went to the rear of the house, but no fruit peddler was in sight. Petite hurried through the back porch and into the hall. And then she saw him! He was standing inside the front door, with his basket at his feet, and he was opening one of the little drawers in Papa's desk!

Afterward, she couldn't remember ever feeling frightened. The first thing she knew, she was facing the peddler, her eyes blazing with anger and both hands clenched into fists. Behind her, Julia stood silent with fear.

"Get your hands off of Papa's desk!" she commanded. "Whatever do you think you're doing?"

Sugar Petite

The peddler shoved the drawer shut with a bang as he turned in surprise. "Why, I . . . I was just shutting the drawer. Someone had left it open." He looked rather sick but attempted an ingratiating smile.

"No one but Papa *ever* touches that desk! He *never* leaves a drawer open; but if he did, it would stay open 'til he shut it himself. Anyway, you have no business coming inside the house and . . . and *stop* smiling at me!" She fairly hurled the words at him. His jaw dropped in response, giving him a very stupid look.

"You're a bad man, and Papa has been waiting for you to come back ever since you sold my little sister that awful cream that nearly ruined her face. He's found out all about you . . . You're not even Mr. Ragusa's cousin like you said. Papa's not here now, but I can tell you for him: Get off this place and don't *ever* come back! If you do, what happens to you will be your own fault!"

His eyes grew large with amazement, and his jaw dropped even lower as the angry little girl continued her tirade: "And don't bother to go to any of the other plantations, either, 'cause they're all goin' to hear about you, and you won't be exactly welcome . . . Now, pick up your basket and get out before I get any madder!"

He didn't have to be told again. Julia said later that the last she saw of him, he was running down the driveway as if something were after him.

"What's the matter?" Mamma's soft voice asked from the bedroom door. "I thought I heard voices."

"Oh, nothing, Mamma dear." Petite had sunk onto the steps with a weak feeling in her knees, but the feeling in her heart was strong and proud. "I was just tending to a piece of business for Papa."

18. Petite Makes a Decision

"Zz-zz-zz." The small, whining song circled high for a moment before the dive-for-attack. Petite lay very still, waiting for the silence and the feather-light pressure on her skin that told her it was time to strike. Then she hit at her forehead with a sharp slap. "Missed it!" she muttered to herself as she heard the shrill, angry sound of retreat. Somehow, in spite of the smoke from Papa's smudge pots and the net mosquito bar completely encircling her bed, one of the pesky creatures had managed to get through to annoy her.

She raised herself on her pillow and deliberately placed both arms outside the sheet to present a tempting field to her enemy. This time she remained motionless until she felt a tiny, sharp jab on one of her arms. Then she slapped again. The slap was followed by complete silence. Her strategy had won the battle.

But now, with the end of the mosquito, the bedroom seemed lonelier than before. Carrie and Lena were still in New Orleans with Papa; and now that the excitement of Charlie's letter had started to fade, she began to think of all the fun she was missing. Mamma had already gone to bed, with little Jenny to keep her company. In the Children's Room the night light was burning; but everything was quiet, which meant that they, too, must have gone to sleep. Brother Jimmie, in his room upstairs, was protection for the family but certainly no company for her. There were no two ways about it—she was lonesome!

Moreover, it was too hot to sleep. It was one of those

Sugar Petite

torrid, humid nights when the air hung so heavy it seemed drawn with difficulty into the lungs. It forced its oppressive weight against her body, making the slightest movement appear an effort. The sharp, stinging odor of the smoking tar and sawdust only added to the feeling of discomfort.

Petite fanned herself with the sheet and then threw it back to the foot of the bed, stretching herself in widespread position to take advantage of as much air as possible. If only Lena were here to talk with her until she felt like going to sleep!

She wanted to show Lena the letter and ask her opinion about what it said. She hadn't dared show it to Mamma, and confiding in Eva was out of the question. There were some things that could only be understood by someone your own age . . . She thought of the girls she had known during her brief stay at school. They had all had secrets which they discussed in small groups during the noon hour and at recess periods. She had never felt a part of the world in which they lived, but now . . . A little thrill of excitement started at the back of her neck and running the length of her body, ended with an ecstatic wiggling of her toes. It could all be hers again for the asking. All she had to do was to tell Papa she really wanted to go back. But this time she must be sure. There could be no turning back once the decision was made.

It seemed so long ago, that Thanksgiving afternoon when she had asked him how she could know when she was really old enough to face life away from home. What were some of the things he had told her?

"*Maybe someday you'll discover that people are leaning on you and depending on you for help*" . . . She

Petite Makes a Decision

thought of Pinkie and the way she had calmed his fears and left him sleeping as quietly as a child, after he had sent for her in the middle of the night. She remembered the tone of Papa's voice, the day of the hurricane, when he asked her to take care of Mamma for him . . .

"*Maybe some difficult situation will arise and you will find yourself handling it alone as a grown person would*" . . . A picture of the fruit peddler flashed across her mind, and she smiled at the memory of how he had gathered up his basket and fled down the steps when she told him to leave. She had felt frightened after it was all over, but at the time it was happening, she had acted without a moment's hesitation as to what she should do . . .

"*Maybe you'll just discover one day that you're thinking like a grownup, enjoying being quiet and alone with your own thoughts*" . . . The peaceful quiet of the tree house, with the children left behind at play; the happy moments alone on the gallery, watching the trees in the moonlight . . .

"*Maybe a real attractive boy will come along, and you'll decide right then that you want to stop being a little girl*" . . . Charlie thought she looked even older than thirteen. He thought she was old enough for him to ask her to be his girl. And he was going off to school and was already full of plans for his life as a doctor. Suppose . . .

She sat up and pulled aside the mosquito bar. She knew now, without a doubt, what she wanted to do; and the wonderful news of the decision strained at her throat, wanting to be told. Perhaps Mamma was still awake.

She slid from the bed and tiptoed to the door. The room was dimly lighted by moonlight but she couldn't

Sugar Petite

see her mother's face. She could only hear her breathing —the slow, heavy breathing of one deep in slumber— and, in the baby bed, the more rapid, short little breaths of Baby Jenny.

Past them and into the Children's Room she softly crept until she reached the side of Julia's cot. "Julia," she whispered. "Julia, are you asleep?" She hadn't bothered to find out first. She must have someone to listen to her, and waking Julia was better than disturbing Mamma.

"Huh?" asked Julia sleepily, sitting up with a yawn. "Oh, it's you, Petite. What's de mattah?"

"Sh! Don't wake anybody! I'm lonesome, and I want you to come in my room and talk to me. I have something to tell you, and I can't go to sleep until I do."

"All right," agreed Julia with a patient sigh. "Ah'll come."

Petite returned to her room and climbed back in bed. A moment later Julia was beside her, carrying the night light which she placed on the bedside table after quietly closing the door behind her. She was wearing one of Mamma's old dressing gowns. It was too large for her and, together with the sleepy expression on her half-lighted face, it gave her a very childish look. Petite suddenly felt much older than she, in spite of the fact that their age was exactly the same.

"Julia," she began, "How do you think you'd like being married to a doctor?"

"Me?" asked Julia in amazement. "Married to a doctah? Now, Petite, you know dere ain't no cullud doctahs!"

"No, silly, not you, of course . . . I mean *anybody*. I wonder what it would feel like having a husband who

Petite Makes a Decision

could make people well and fix 'em up inside when there's something wrong with them, and all . . ."

"Petite, you ain't thinkin' about gittin' *married?*" There was a note of horror in Julia's voice.

"Certainly not. Not now, at least, but I was just thinking . . . a doctor's wife would have to know lot's of things. Julia, I've decided something. I really want to go back to New Orleans to school next year!"

There was a moment of silence. Then, "You ain't gonna be homesick no more?"

"Oh, maybe so," said Petite casually. "Everybody gets a little homesick, I guess. But soon you get so interested in everything you forget all about it. And . . . and you just have to get away from home for a while sometime, or else you'll never learn to stand on your own feet and make your own decisions and all . . . You've got to face the world someday."

"Oh." Julia said it in a very small voice, and then she said nothing. She stood beside the bed, holding together the ill-fitting gown, her soft, dark eyes studying the carpet beneath her feet.

"Don't you think so?" asked Petite.

"Ah reckon so. It . . . it do sound right."

"*She doesn't understand a word I'm saying,*" thought Petite. "*It's all outside her world. I can't talk to her after all.*"

What happened then seemed so real Petite felt that she could almost reach out and touch it. It was like a great wall sliding slowly between her and the slight, brown girl who had always been one of her closest friends; between the happy childhood that had been hers and the thrilling uncertainty of the years that lay ahead. Perhaps she could hold it back if she tried, but she had no desire to do so. This was the way it must be, and there was no longer any feeling of resistance in her heart.

"Thank you for coming, Julia," she said kindly. "I just wanted to tell you . . . and now I think I want to go to sleep."

Julia picked up the night light. She didn't speak again until she reached the door. Then she turned and looked wistfully toward the bed. "Goodnight, *Miss Pearl*," she said slowly.

Petite lay back on the pillow. One of her fingers sought the pearl in Papa's Christmas ring. *Miss Pearl!* It had a beautiful sound. It was a beautiful name, and tomorrow would be a beautiful day . . . "Goodnight, Julia," she answered.

Epilogue

Petite grew up to marry her Doctor Charlie after many years of waiting. The gypsy's predictions came true: "A long life, a happy life, a life of loving others and making them happy." At the time when this book was first published she was eighty-seven years old, inactive but still in good health. She was honored at a *Sugar Petite* reception and smilingly greeted the guests with a corsage made of sugar cubes pinned at her shoulder and a copy of her story held in her hands. She lived on for several more years, surrounded by the love of her three children and the six adoring grandchildren mentioned in the Foreword. Today there are thirteen great-grandchildren added to the number, to finish out the future foretold by the gypsy so many years ago.

Songs and Games From Belle Vale

Of all the broken bits of Belle Vale tradition, the songs and games recalled from childhood hold the greatest appeal to the listeners. Doubtless many have been lost forever. Of the few remaining ones here recorded, most of them were apparently learned from the plantation servants. Indeed several seem to be entirely unique, with the possibility that they may have been composed by the Negroes themselves or have been their own variations of the folk songs familiar to them. An example of this is the song, "Juba," which has no evident meaning at all but, nonetheless, was and still is a favorite with all who hear it. The theory is a likely one that it may have had its origin in African "voodoo" or Black Magic, with its weird, chanting rhythm and its mention of killing the "yaller cat."

JUBA

She grind de meal,
She gimme de husk.
She bake de bread,
She gimme de crust.
Juba, Juba,
Juba dis an' Juba dat,
Juba killed de yaller cat.
Ole Aunt Kate!

The verse is chanted in a low monotone, the last word pronounced as two syllables with the voice raised about two notes at the end.

Songs and Games from Belle Vale

GO TELL AUNT TABBY

Go tell Aunt Tabby, go tell Aunt Tabby
Go tell Aunt Tabby de ole gray goose is dead.
De one dat she was savin', de one dat she was savin'
De one dat she was savin' to make a feather bed.
Now pore Aunt Tabby, Now pore Aunt Tabby,
Now pore Aunt Tabby won't have her feather bed.

Sugar Petite

DOWN MOBILE

1.

Miss Chippy-Chappy jump out-a bed,
She run to de winder an' poke out her head.
A snowball hit her in de eye-ball—Bim!
Look-a-here, little darkie, don't you do dat agin!

Chorus:
Down Mobile, down Mobile,
How Ah love dem pretty-eyed gals
Down Mobile.

2.

Ah gotta a gal, she's 'leven feet tall;
She sleeps in de kitchen wid her feet in de hall.
She gotta sister across de lake
Can shake de shimmy like a wicked rattle snake.

(Chorus)

Songs and Games from Belle Vale

3.

De biggest fool Ah ever saw
Jes' got back from Arkansas.
He wore his shirt outside his coat
An' buckled his pants up 'round his throat.
(Chorus)

4.

Ole Aunt Dinah, she got drunk,
She fell in de fire an' she kick up a chunk.
A red hot coal got in her shoe
An' Oh, Lawd-a-mussy, how de ashes flew!
(Chorus)

5.

Mah Massa's gotta great big house,
It's sixteen stories high,
An ev'ry room in Massa's house
Is filled wid chicken pie.
(Chorus)

6.

Way down yonder in Beaver Creek
Where dem darkies grow 'leven feet,
Ev'y time dey goes to bed
Dere feet sticks out an' dere heads turn red.
(Chorus)

7.

Ah know sumpin' Ah ain't gonna tell—
Three little babies in a peanut shell.
One can read an' one can write
An' one can smoke his daddy's pipe.
(Chorus)

Sugar Petite

OLE AUNT JEMIMY

2.

Jes' listen dat fuss is a-makin' upstairs,
(Ole Aunt Jemimy, pore ole soul!)
'Tain't nothin' but a rooster sayin' his prayers.
(Ole Aunt Jemimy, pore ole soul!)

(Chorus)

3.

Ah crep' to de hen house on mah knees,
(Ole Aunt Jemimy, pore ole soul!)
Ah thought Ah heard a chicken sneeze.
(Ole Aunt Jemimy, pore ole soul!)

(Chorus)

Songs and Games from Belle Vale
BIG-EYE RABBIT

Ah went to de East an' Ah went to de West
An' Ah went to No'th Ca'lina,
An' de purtiest gal Ah saw while gone
Was Big-Eye Rabbit's daughter.

Big-Eye Rabbit, shoo, shoo!
Big-Eye Rabbit, shoo, boy!
Big-Eye Rabbit, shoo, shoo!
An' de Lord above us bless you.

Gotta pain in mah fingah,
Gotta pain in mah toe,
But mah ole Missus call me
So Ah mus' go.

Sugar Petite
WHAR YOU GOIN', BUZZARD?

Whar you goin', Buzzard?
Whar you goin', Crow?
Goin' down to New Groun' to jump Jim Crow.
Me an' my missus an' two or three mo',
Ev'y time us turns aroun'
Us doos jes' so
An' us doos jes' so
An' us doos jes' so!

The last three lines are acted out with a flapping motion of the shoulders and arms, the singer turning his body from side to side to represent a bird dancing and flapping its wings.

Songs and Games from Belle Vale
ALL ROUND THE ROSE BUSH

All round the rose bush,
Just like a posey,
Come all my pretty little playmates
And take a seat by me.
Miss (Jenny) she loves sugar and tea,
Miss (Jenny) she loves candy,
Miss (Jenny) she can turn around
And kiss the one comes handy.

The children, holding hands, form a ring and, with everyone singing, walk around one child who has been chosen to be "It" and stands in the center. Upon the line, "And take a seat by me," everyone sits down except "It," who chooses one child out of the circle and takes her into the center, holding both of her hands and pulling her back and forth during the next two lines. With the last two lines, "It" spins her around and she must kiss the nearest child in the circle, this child then becomes "It" and the other two taking a place in the ring.

Sugar Petite

CHICKAMA, CHICKAMA, CRANEY-CROW

Chickama, Chickama, Craney-Crow,
Ah went to de well to wash mah toe
When Ah got back mah chicken was gone.
What time, ole witch?

There is some difference of opinion as to just how this game was played, but the procedure was probably something like this:

One child, chosen to be the witch, stood in the center of a ring formed by the other children, who had previously decided upon a certain time of the clock. They marched around the witch, holding hands and reciting the above verse. After the question, "What time, ole witch?" the old witch guessed a time. If it was not correct, the children repeated the circling and singing. If she happened to guess the correct time, they all broke hands and ran, the old witch trying to catch one of them who would then take her place in the center of the ring.

Songs and Games from Belle Vale

WILLIAM COME TRIMMLE TOE

William Come Trimmle Toe,
He's a good fisherman.
Catches his hens, puts 'em in pens;
Some lay eggs an' some lay none.
Wire, briar, limber lock,
Three geese in a flock,
One flew East, an' one flew West
An' one flew over the cuckoo's nest.
O-U-T spells OUT!

Procedure of Game

The first part of the game, given above, proceeds like any "count out" game, the person counting out the other children becoming the "Questioner" for the rest of the game. The last one to be counted out is "It" and leaves the room. Each of the remaining children chooses a name for himself (animals, birds, flowers, etc., the names usually being within one group). A name is also chosen for the child who has gone out. After the child who is "It" is called back to the door of the room, the following dialogue takes place between him and the Questioner:

> Question: "When you comin' home?"
> Answer: "Tomorrow afternoon."
> Question: "What you gonna bring?"
> Answer: "A dish an' a spoon an' a fat raccoon."
> Question: "What'd you rather come on?" (Names all the chosen names.)
> Answer: "It" decides on one name. Whoever is named must go to the door and carry "It" in on his back. If he has chosen his own name, he must come in on tip-toe.

Sugar Petite

Question: "What you got there?"
Answer: (Answered by the one carrying "It"): "A bag of fleas."
Question: "Shake 'em 'til they sneeze."
The one carrying "It" shakes him until he sneezes: "Katchoo," upon which he is let down.
Question: "What'd you rather fall on, a thorn bed or a feather bed?"
"It" chooses one. If the answer is " A thorn bed," he is instructed to "Fall down easy"; if "A feather bed," to "Fall down *hard!*"

This is the end of the game. The one who has been "It" becomes the Questioner, who counts out the other children, and the game is repeated from the beginning.

Belle Vale Family Records

Papa

JAMES LOUIS Lobdell
Born February 16, 1833
Married July 30, 1857, to Angelina Adelia Bird
Died September 19, 1886

Mamma

ANGELINA ADELIA Bird
Born June 14, 1842
Married July 30, 1857, to James Louis Lobdell
Died December 17, 1929

Children

JOHN Bird Lobdell
Born July 30, 1858
Married December 22, 1881, to Elizabeth Handy Randolph
Died January 1899
Children:
Josephine (Josie) Randolph Lobdell m. Dr. David Allen Berwick
Elizabeth (Lizzie) Randolph Lobdell m. John Calhoun Blackman
John Randolph Lobdell; unmarried

Mary BELLE Lobdell
Born September 13, 1860
Married June 14, 1883, to Edward Finley Phillips
Died September 8, 1897

Belle Vale Family Records

Children:
- Angie Lena Phillips m. Thomas Buffington Brown
- Marshall Pope Phillips m. Margaret Flynn
- Gertrude Olivia Phillips m. Edgar Ray Weiland

James (JIMMIE) Louis Lobdell, Jr.
Born September 7, 1863
Married September 5, 1888, to Amelie Marie Rouzan
Died March 31, 1897
Children:
- Lena; died at 17 months
- James Louis Lobdell III; unmarried
- Cyril Rouzan Lobdell m. Gertrude Altazin

CARRIE Louise Lobdell
Born December 20, 1865
Married February 16, 1887, to John Little Lobdell
Died August 15, 1926
Children:
- Anne Lobdell m. Armstead Richardson Kilbourne
- Belle Lobdell; unmarried
- John Little Lobdell, Jr., m. Hazel Cook

Angelina (LENA) Julia Lobdell
Born October 29, 1869
Married September 27, 1888, to John Hermann Matta
Died December 22, 1966
Children:
- La Noue Matta m. Marie Stewart
- Eugenia Ruth Matta m. Rodney Charlton Hardin

PEARL ("Petite') Winnifred Lobdell
Born September 5, 1871
Married February 5, 1894, to Dr. Charles McVea, Sr.
Died August 8, 1962

Belle Vale Family Records

Children:
Pearl McVea m. Ivy Laurence Morris
Dr. Charles McVea, Jr., m. Mildred Frances Lamoreaux
Bena McVea m. John Alexander (Jac) Chambliss, Jr.

EVA May Lobdell
   Born September 5, 1875
   Married September 5, 1900, to Harrison (Hal) Custis
      Bradford
   Died October 4, 1946
   Child:
      Harrison C. Bradford, Jr., m. Hallie

Lavenia (BENA) Bird Lobdell
   Born January 17, 1878
   Married January 4, 1897, to Marcus Page Exline
   Died August 8, 1910
   Children:
      Albert Lobdell Exline m. Emma Jennings Miller
      Bena Louise Exline m. William Hudson Philps
      Dorothy Dunlap Exline m. Ralph Emerson Fair
      Marcus Page Exline, Jr., m. Chrystelle Houten

William (NOOTSIE) Abraham Lobdell
   Born October 14, 1882
   Married July 25, 1906, to Virginia (Jennie) Young (d.1924)
   Married September 18, 1926, to Eleanor Cabell
   Died August 31, 1947
   Children:
      William Young Lobdell; died as an infant
      William Young (Bill) Lobdell m. Elizabeth Barrett
         Hustmyre
      Virginia Adelia Lobdell m. Robert Bernard Jennings
      Warren Russell Lobdell; died in World War II
      Eva Mae Lobdell; died at 11 months
      Eleanor Lobdell m. Coleman L. McVea

Belle Vale Family Records

JENNIE (Jayne) Lydia Lobdell
   Born June 29, 1886
   Married June 18, 1914, to Charles Vernon Porter, Jr.
   Died June 28, 1966
   Children:
      Unnamed son; died at birth
      Jane Lobdell Porter m. Frank Walters Middleton, Jr.